# *At Fortunoff's*
## and Other Stories

## Miguel Antonio Ortiz

**H\S**
Hamilton Stone Editions
Maplewood, New Jersey

Cover Design by Adalberto Ortiz

Library of Congress Cataloging-in-Publication Data

Ortiz, Miguel Antonio.
  [Short stories. Selections]
  At Fortunoff 's and other stories / by Miguel Antonio Ortiz.
    pages ; cm
  ISBN 978-0-9836668-6-8 (alk. paper)
  1. New York (N.Y.)--Fiction. I. Ortiz, Miguel Antonio. At
Fortunoff's. II. Title.
  PS3615.R825A6 2014
  813'.6--dc23
                              2014013481

# Contents

At Fortunoff's / 5
Camila / 16
Dark from the Tap / 29
Reader and Adviser / 37
Joanie / 52
Rachel or Diane? / 72
Separate Lives / 82
An Occupied Bench / 95
Literary Affairs / 109
Modern Art / 125
Rosamaria / 133
The Desk / 143
The Call / 161
Sale at Barney's / 164
Thursday Night / 169
Chicken Curry / 174

# At Fortunoff's

*F*ROM BEHIND HIS desk at the Inwood Publishing Company, Mario caught glimpses of Jacqueline as she moved about her office across from his. He found her look of innocence attractive, though aware of the possibility that it was the product of his imagination, and she was in fact teasing him. A diamond sparkled prominently from her hand, a sure sign that it was safe to flirt with her. She was only twenty-one years old. He was fifteen years older and had acquired an assurance he lacked when younger. He was no longer afraid of the unknown, or at least the part irrelevant to everyday life. He was willing to ignore the greater mysteries of the universe and approach the world with some assurance.

Having noticed his gaze, she walked over to his office. "Will you go with me to Fortunoff's at lunchtime?" she asked.

"Sure," he said.

"You don't mind, really?"

"Really, I don't."

"You can help me pick out linen," she said. "I have to do all these things before my wedding."

"It's getting close, isn't it?"

"Yes, I'm getting nervous."

"Cold feet?"

"No, not really," she said, "I'm just getting nervous."

"Everything will be all right."

"You've been married a long time, haven't you?" she said.

"Ten years."

"And you've survived."

"Yes, I'm still here."

"And you're happy?"

"I'm happy," he said.

At Fortunoff's they looked at the linens, but there was nothing she liked. He followed her as she sauntered over to the jewelry counter. The salesperson, her face loaded with makeup, approached them. "May I show you something?" she asked. She was very young, perhaps younger than Jacqueline. Mario appreciated that Jacqueline used makeup sparingly. What was the use of a face that had to be scraped off every night and reapplied every morning? Women who did that were alien to him, as if they were from a different tribe whose customs were exotic and incomprehensible. But he did sometimes flirt with the secretary in the oversized book department, who swore she wouldn't step out of the house without applying her full set of war paint. She even tried every morning to keep her husband from seeing her before her mask was on. Presumably, at night they made love before she took it off, or they always turned off the light before facing each other.

"Oh, no," Jacqueline said. "We're just browsing."

"Well, I see you have the essentials," the salesperson said, looking at Jacqueline's diamond ring. "You know how to pick out jewelry," she said to Mario.

He was about to correct her, but was prevented by a yank on his arm. "Oh yes, he's quite good at it," Jacqueline said.

After they left the jewelry counter he tried to explain, "She thought it was us, that I'm your fiancé."

"I know what she thought," Jacqueline said. "Let her think it. Let's pretend for a little while. Can you handle that?" There was a gentle mockery in her voice as well as at the corners of her smile.

He would be all right if he could keep himself from blushing, and if his pulse would subside. "I think I can handle it," he said, even as he felt the lack of spittle in his mouth for a moment.

"All right," she said as she dragged him towards housewares, where she spied wicker baskets that appealed to her. "Do you like these?" she asked.

"They're fine," he said.

"No, really, do you like them a lot?"

"They're fine," he repeated, "but I'm not the one who's going to live with them."

"You're not getting into the spirit of this," she said. "It's just a game."

"Okay," he said.

"I'm going to buy these baskets."

"I think you should."

She picked out three different sized baskets. At the register the salesperson said, "These are great. They come in very handy." Before they left she wished them luck. This time Mario managed to be gracious. "Thank you," he said.

"That wasn't so bad, was it?" Jacqueline said.

"I suppose not," Mario conceded. "No use swimming against the current."

"It's not as if you were in any danger of drowning," she responded.

"Yes, it's only a game," he said.

"Let's take a cab," she suggested. "It's too unwieldy to carry these baskets on the bus."

"We can take the subway," he said.

She insisted on the cab, and at the curb signaled for one. She gave the driver her home address.

"We're not going back to work?" Mario inquired.

"We have plenty of time," she said, "no one will miss us."

"Not even Kotmier?"

Kotmier, a short man with a bushy moustache that drooped slightly over the corners of his mouth, ran the oversized books department. A bald spot was beginning to emerge at the crown of his head, and perhaps that accounted for the perpetually sad look that emanated from his brown eyes. Despite his unpromising looks, he was married to a very attractive woman. His wife did not only play the vivacious blond, but was also a proper and gracious lady when the occasion demanded. It was the consensus among his colleagues that Kotmier had lucked out when he married, but the same could not be said for his wife. A woman like Mrs. Kotmier could have done better. It was easier to solve the Rubik's cube than to figure out what she saw in him. There was no discernible flaw in her to explain such a lapse in judgment. Consequently a suspicion lingered, ever unproven, that Kotmier possessed a hidden quality that compensated for his outward demeanor.

Kotmier, however, had begun to show signs that he did not appreciate his position. He had begun to pay undue attention to Jacqueline. She was used to attention from men, and didn't think anything of it until he showed up at her door early one morning before work.

"Oh, what a surprise," she said.

"I was just passing by, and I thought you might want some company on your way to work."

"Oh, sure," she said, "what a great idea, but you might have called first, and I would have been ready to go. Now you'll have to wait."

Later she lamented to Mario, "I don't know why I didn't tell him off right then."

"Well, you were caught off guard. It's hard to say the right thing at an unexpected moment. And you didn't want to hurt his feelings in case he was there for a totally innocent reason, as he said."

"What if Hillary finds out?"

"You didn't do anything wrong."

"Yes, but it wouldn't look like that."

"Just tell him you don't want him to do it any-more, and that will be that."

She told him, and he complied. He didn't ring her doorbell anymore. He would wait for her at the corner, except on the days when Larry, her fiancé, stayed over. Then she and Larry would leave the house together in the morning, and there was no sign of Kotmier.

"How does he know when Larry is staying over? He must be watching me," she said to Mario.

"And what does Larry make of all this?"

"Oh, I haven't told him. I'm afraid to. He might kill Kotmier, and then where would we be?"

"He's got a temper, does he?"

"You could say that, but I try to keep it in check. At a party once, one of his friends came on to me. I mean, it wasn't terrible. He just got too close to me, so I walloped him, mostly just to keep Larry from feeling that he had to retaliate, because he would have killed the guy."

"I suppose a slap on the face is a fair enough price to pay for touching your behind."

"Not everybody has to pay the price," she said.

She crossed in front of him as if to give him an unequivocal view of the merchandise now that he knew the price. His paralysis was beyond his will. How she might interpret his action, or lack of it, became a concern, but he took comfort in the fact that she had no way of knowing its source. Though she sometimes surprised him with the perspicacity of her observations, he was certain that in this case she could only guess. Whether that was enough protection was a question. Her admiration might easily morph into contempt. His concern was allayed over the next few days as he saw no change in her behavior towards him. Neither one of them alluded to the conversation again, as if it had never happened.

A few weeks later an Inwood book was picked up by the Book-of-the-Month Club, producing kudos for Inwood, its publications being primarily specialty books with a limited audience. Occasionally, however, quite incidentally, one of their books, for reasons mysterious to the editors and even more so to the happy author, broke out of its niche and appealed to the literate masses. Those occasions at Inwood traditionally called for a celebration hosted by the editor of the book and open to the whole staff. Usually everyone merely traipsed down after hours to a local bar to have a few drinks and *hors d'oeuvres*.

For most of the evening Jacqueline stayed close to Mario, but eventually she moved away to mix with other colleagues. Kotmier, as if he had been waiting for just such an opportunity, lurched toward Mario. A tendency to be maudlin when inebriated was one of Kotmier's least endearing qualities, and Mario braced himself to hear once again the story of how much Inwood had done for Kotmier, and how he would do anything, short of child abuse, for the company to which he owed his very life. Because of course, a life without intellect was no life at all, and what was Inwood if not a haven of culture and intellect? But this time, Kotmier surprised his victim. "She's a sweet girl, isn't she?" he said pausing between words as if each had to stop and pay a toll at a gate between his teeth.

"Who?" Mario inquired, thinking that Kotmier was referring to the person to whom he was speaking before he had turned to Mario, and whom Mario hadn't noticed.

"Jacqueline," Kotmier said, "of course, I mean Jacqueline."

"Oh, yes of course Jacqueline," how could he be so dense as to not know immediately in a room full of women that "sweet" described only one of them?

"And do you know," Kotmier said sticking his index finger into Mario's chest, "that she's engaged to be married?"

"Yes, I know that," Mario said.

"Yes, you know that," Kotmier reiterated as if this piece of information was totally unexpected and had derailed his train of thought. "And her fiancé, he's a wonderful young man too, as you must know."

"I presume so," Mario said. "I've never met him."

Annoyance momentarily flitted over Kotmier's face. His expectations were not being met, but he was determined to stay on course. "Oh, he is. They make a perfect couple, picture perfect."

"I'm sure they do," Mario concurred.

"And it wouldn't do to spoil such a perfect picture, would it?"

"No it wouldn't."

"So we see eye to eye on this," Kotmier said, having difficulty keeping his balance as he tried to bring his eyes level with Mario's.

"I think you need another drink," Mario said. "It will steady you."

"You're right," Kotmier said, and he lurched away in the direction of the bar.

Later, when the import of that conversation bobbed to the surface of Mario's awareness, he didn't know whether to be concerned or whether to laugh. He did a little of both, but he never mentioned it to Jacqueline. It would have been awkward to say, "You know, Kotmier thinks we're having an affair," maybe because they both knew that their having lunch together every day had been noted by everyone else in the office. Although no one said anything to them directly, it would have been unreasonable to assume the absence of gossip.

He recalled the conversation with Kotmier as he rode in the taxi towards Jacqueline's apartment. She had pressed up close to him to make room for the baskets. Putting the baskets between them might have been more convenient, but then he would have missed having her body close to his and being overwhelmed by the smell of her hair. He gratifyingly imagined Kotmier's chagrin on seeing them sitting close together in a taxi and heading towards her apartment where they would be alone even if only for a few minutes. He was puzzled as to why he saw Kotmier as a rival, while not giving any thought at all to Larry, who presumably was the beneficiary of her affection, and who would soon have an even greater claim to what he now enjoyed through magnanimity.

Kotmier was a physical presence, while Larry was a shadow, known only through hearsay. Mario had constructed a caricature of Larry, the young medical student with a parochial view of the world. "He says that my salary will be the play money when we're married," Jacqueline had proudly informed him. Mario wanted to shake her, to shout at her, "Don't fall into that trap. You're too good for that." But it wasn't his place to do that; a rescue was only possible through an intimate partnership. He was already committed somewhere else. She would have to save herself. He had faith in her. She was strong enough and smart enough to do it.

An antiseptic elegance pervaded Jacqueline's apartment, its thoroughly modern decor simultaneously chilling and engrossing—glass and chrome her favorite materials. As soon as he walked in, the unexpected surprised him, though he couldn't have said exactly what he had expected, only that it differed from what he saw. Dashes of color leapt out with startling effect, though closer inspection revealed the object to be quite muted, and only its place in the overall setting made it seem dramatic. Jacqueline moved about in contrast to the surroundings. The sparse and cold decor failed to reflect who she was. He did not, even for a moment, consider that he didn't know her well enough to judge.

"Just put the baskets down anywhere," she said. "Relax, look around. Do you like the place?"

"It's not you," he said.

"Lots of people say that," she retorted. "It must be a hidden part of me."

"Maybe there's a reason for hiding it," he said.

"You're becoming disillusioned with me," she said. She had meant it as a joke, but it came out closer to regret, and anxiety tinged the smile on her lips.

"Not possible," he flippantly retorted.

She knew that he had not stopped to consider what his words meant, so she asked him, "Because you have no illusions about me, or because you'll hold on to them at any cost?"

"What are you talking about?"

"I have smoked turkey in the refrigerator. Why don't I make us sandwiches, and we won't have to stop somewhere else to eat," she said.

"Good idea," he said. "I'll help you with the sandwiches."

"All right," she said, "I'll put up the coffee."

He was glad to be doing something other than thinking about the remark that had startled him. Being so closely observed was less than comfortable. He wondered whether he was as obvious as a child, or whether she was uncommonly insightful. He preferred the latter. He sensed her retreat, her leaving the next step entirely up to him. At the edge of the precipice, he had to make a decision.

They ate the sandwiches in silence.

"We better head back," he said as soon as they had finished.

"Yes, we better. I'll clean up later," she said.

In the foyer, before they stepped out into the street, she kissed him lightly on the cheek. "I'm sorry," she said.

"No need," he replied, "the sandwiches were really good."

"Yes, they were," she said.

# Camila

"*A* NEW PLACE!" she exclaimed pirouetting around her living room imagining an apartment completely different from the one she was in.

Sheldon looked up trying to fathom what all the excitement was about. He gave Camila a long quizzical look, and failing to note anything of immediate import, he opened his mouth in a wide yawn, raised his rear end, extended his two front paws, and after giving himself a long stretch, he ambled away in search of a more peaceful spot.

"So! Walking away from me, are you?" she exclaimed. She swooped down on him before he could dash under the couch. Her hand under his belly, she brought him up to her face, and looking him straight in the eyes, she told him what laid in store for them both in the very near future. "So you see, Sheldon, we're going to move whether you like it or not. I know you've gotten used to this place, but I've made up my mind, and there's no use arguing with me. I know you. You make a fuss now, but later you'll act as if it had been your idea to move."

Not wanting to face up to that particular flaw in his character, Sheldon turned his head away. He stuck his tongue out to wipe his face. His mistress, seeing that he was in one of his haughty moods, and knowing that he would be wryly disdainful of anything she said at the moment, deposited him back on the green carpeting. He scurried towards the door and began to meow.

"Hush, Sheldon," she said. "Don't you have any manners?"

Sheldon ignored her. Over the din, Camila heard the jingling of keys and the tumbler of the lock turning. The muscles of her face tightened, and her shoulders contracted.

Roberto greeted Sheldon but scarcely said a word to Camila. He went straight to the kitchen where he put up water for tea.

"I haven't seen you in days," she said, following him into the kitchen. "How are you?"

"I'm all right," he said, darting a glance at her.

"How's Mary Anne?"

"All right," he mechanically said.

"Aren't you living with her now?"

"Why this sudden interest in Mary Anne?" he queried, a wave of emotion rippling over his face.

"Just curious," she said trying to seem nonchalant.

"You're sure?"

"Actually, it's not just curiosity," she answered, but her thoughts became muddled, and she forgot what she wanted to say. There was a long pause.

"What is it then?" he asked, still avoiding her face.

"I was thinking that if you're living with Mary Anne, you can take your stuff out of here. This apartment is too small, and your things are in my way. I mean, I can't keep them here forever, can I?"

He didn't respond immediately, but merely stared at the water in the pot. "I'm not living with Mary Anne, and I don't plan to," he said.

"Well, wherever, you have to take your things out of here."

"I will," he said.

"I really mean it this time," she said.

"I'm going to," he reiterated, "as soon as I find a permanent place."

"I don't want to wait indefinitely," she said. "I want you to get everything out of here by tomorrow night." Never before having been so definite, her own words startled her.

"Are you crazy?" he sneered. "That's not enough time."

"And another thing," she continued, "I don't want you dropping in here unannounced. Well, I mean, I have rights too, after all, this is my apartment." Her eyes were now pleading for understanding.

"You want some tea?" he asked.

He took her lack of response as an affirmative, and fetching two cups from the cupboard, placed a tea bag in each and poured the water.

She accepted the cup, sipped the tea, and felt fortified as the warm liquid flowed down her throat. "I'm sorry if I'm being hard on you. But I can't go on like this."

"It doesn't have to be this way," he said.

"That's right, it doesn't, and now it's going to change."

"It could be the way it used to be."

"No, it can't. The way it used to be was terrible."

"It wasn't always."

"Yes, it was. It was terrible from the very beginning."

"Then why did you let it go on?"

She looked at him disdainfully, and brought the cup of tea to her lips. Why was he putting her through this? She wanted him to leave without making a fuss, without making her explain. After she drained the last drop in the cup, by way of dismissal she said, "I have to go to work now."

He didn't move from his seat until she disappeared into the bedroom. He followed her. She proceeded to lay out her clothes to dress for work. He moved closer to her and placed his hand on her bare shoulder.

"Stop that, Roberto!"

"You're not human," he said. In a melodramatic gesture, he clasped his hands to his head and collapsed on the bed, but seeing that Camila's patience was at the point of exhaustion, he picked himself up and left, slamming the front door behind him.

Panic overwhelmed her. In search of an anchor, she looked around the room. She focused on the framed photograph of a young man that rested on her dresser. He was tall and thin and sported a wide smile, the very image of collegiate cleverness, the sort of young man who might have stepped out of the pages of F. Scott Fitzgerald. That young man in the photograph was certainly capable of love. She was sure of that. She remembered ambling through the park with him and seeing his shadow extend ahead of them. There was something to this dark entity, a magical extension of that physical being that took her for walks before the retreat of the sun transformed the sky with the warm colors of the evening. She remembered playing the game of not wanting to go to bed. He would swoop her into his arms and carry her to her bedroom, where he tucked her into bed and bent down to kiss her forehead while she extended her arms around his neck to hold him there as long as possible, longing to force him down into the bed beside her. He had loved her when she was a child. Yes, she was sure of that. She held on to that thought until she was calm enough to continue dressing.

§

Taking a break from the daily routine of reading manuscripts, at her desk, Camila sat talking to one her of her colleagues at the Inwood Publishing Company.

"Just the other day, I went to see a psychic," Camila said very nonchalantly.

Her colleague, a young man, stared curiously at her. "Did you?" he asked.

For a moment she wondered whether he doubted what she had just said, or whether he was merely trying to disguise his astonishment. She really didn't want him to think that she was in any way abnormal, but merely wished that she could make everyone understand who she really was.

"I had questions about my mother," she said. "She's a frightening woman. I was always terrified of her."

"You mean, she abused you?"

"Well, it all depends on what you mean by that. She didn't beat me, or anything, but she didn't love me either. She had awesome power," Camila continued, "power to do harm. In a previous life she was a witch. That's what the psychic told me, and I believe it. I'm sure she still has some of the power she had in that previous life."

"You think she would use such powers against you—her own daughter?"

"She never liked me. She was always jealous of me, because I was my father's favorite. He liked me best, better than he liked her. At least when I was a child, he liked me. He doesn't very much like women, and he never liked her."

"He must have loved her once," the young man said. "He courted her. Didn't he?"

"He married her for her money. It's a terrible thing to have money."

"Then we lucked out, didn't we? "

She gazed at him, wondering whether he thought her strange, and a bundle of contradictions. She had impressed him, he once told her, by her intellectualism. She supposed that he was referring to her having attended prestigious schools. She wasn't exactly beautiful, so her looks couldn't be quite what impressed him. Nevertheless, she could tell that he was attracted to her, that he didn't mind the thick texture of her hair, her puffy cheeks and a chin that came to point. When she examined her body in the mirror, she always concluded that she had wide hips, and she rued her inability to quite fill out the seat of her pants. Still, the vibes emanating from the young man assured her of her sexual attraction.

Another time she told him about her first encounter with Roberto. "When I woke up in the morning, there was a stranger in bed with me, and I was surprised, until I remembered that at the party the night before, I had mistaken him for someone else. I thought it was safe enough to flirt with him, since he was already attached to my friend Emiliana. I was just having a lark for a few minutes to pass the time, but I had made a mistake."

Of course, when she was explaining this, it didn't make any sense. Emiliana and her boyfriend, Charles, had walked over to her as she sat at the corner of the couch under the lamp light.

"Charles, this is Camila," Emiliana had said.

Camila turned to the person with whom she had been exercising her coquettish charm and asked, "And who are you?"

"Roberto," he said. "Very pleased to meet you."

For a few seconds she was somewhat flustered, but she quickly recovered. She believed in Fate, and so she ascribed this incidental occurrence to the workings of a higher power. Her mistaking Roberto for someone else and letting down her guard had to be more meaningful than it first appeared.

She stayed with him for the rest of the evening, as if the mistake had created an attachment that she lacked the power to undo.

But perhaps the chance meeting wasn't what promoted her action, but rather his emotional state. He claimed that the meaninglessness of life had overwhelmed him. He needed a reason to stay alive and continue the struggle. The woman he had been seeing for several months had bewitched him in some way beyond his power to resist, he said. Camila knew such machinations were possible. Such women existed in the world. She knew that first hand.

As he spoke, she realized that something had begun. At the party that night, he proceeded to drink a great deal and was somewhat tipsy when she took him home with her. As they ascended the stairs to her place, he tripped on one of the steps and banged his knee. Once in the apartment, she retrieved the ice pack from the freezer, and she applied it to the bruised knee. She helped the inebriated figure into bed expecting nothing further, but he suddenly became aroused. She had been quite satisfied with just taking care of him. In fact, that's what satisfied her most, that she was there for some helpless person who needed her.

§

After work, Camila walked cross-town to Emiliana's. She did not call ahead but took a chance that her friend would be home; figuring that in any event the walk would be pleasant. She was gratified to find her friend at home. At Emiliana's, she felt enveloped by a sense of well-being, and she began to look more favorably on what she usually considered clutter. The clashing bright colors and the haphazard arrangement of odds and ends revealed the lack of appreciation of coherence.

"I hope you don't mind my barging in on you like this," Camila said.

"I don't mind at all. Don't be silly," Emiliana responded, in her small breathy voice. "Sit down in this nice comfy chair," she continued, as she pointed to an armchair of maternal proportions. "You don't look well at all."

"I don't know what's the matter with me," Camila said.

"Well, to tell the truth, I'm not feeling exactly terrific myself," Emiliana commiserated.

A wave of concern suddenly swept over Camila like sleep on a tired person trying to stay awake, drooping for a few seconds and then sitting up with a start only to doze off again.

"I may lose my job anytime now," Emiliana said. "Funds are being cut from my department."

Camila listened, but the words seemed to slide off her consciousness without making an impression. A vague voice seemed to be telling her that there was nothing she could do about Emiliana's problem, but that voice too was scarcely audible. Suddenly, she regained lucidity, and remembered what she wanted to discuss, what had brought her to Emiliana's. But Emiliana's voice completely filled the room, forcing Camila to keep quiet. She mused on the phenomenon of her friend's voice, ordinarily so small and delicate, suddenly becoming overwhelming.

"I guess I can collect unemployment," Emiliana said.

Camila again tried to recall what she had come to discuss. Oh, yes, an apartment, that was it.

"Yes," Emiliana continued, "but I guess it can be worse."

What can be worse than listening to Emiliana? But fearing that she might lose control of her tongue, Camila reproached herself. She had been harsh with Roberto that morning. There was no helping that. She had been forced to do that. There was no need, however, to be unpleasant with Emiliana. She told herself that she didn't love Roberto. She could not explain to herself, and much less to anyone else, why she had allowed him into her life.

"I think I'm going to move," Camila said.

"Move? Leave New York?"

"No, of course not," Camila replied trying to keep her annoyance at Emiliana's simplicity under control. "I just need a different apartment."

"Rents are incredible, and you have such a nice place," Emiliana said.

"Well, I'm tired of it."

"Yes, I can understand that," Emiliana said, trying to be agreeable.

No, you don't. You don't understand at all, because I haven't told you why I really want to move. Of course, I don't really know either, do I? Her mind flashed to the apartment filled with furniture she didn't like. It was Roberto's taste. She had let him convince her to buy all that glass and chrome she hated.

"Maybe I can get rid of Roberto along with the apartment," she said. "He's almost a fixture anyway."

"Ah, Roberto, is he still around?" The question was meant to convey information rather than solicit any. Emiliana's turn had arrived to note the oddness of her friend. "If all you want is to get rid of Roberto, why don't you just throw him out, and he can take the furniture with him? That's a lot simpler than moving."

Seeing the futility of discussing the matter with Emiliana, Camila stood up to leave and escape her friend's insipidness.

Close to home, she spied Larry, her upstairs neighbor, walking a few yards ahead of her. He was apparently returning from the library. He held his books on his arm with their bottom edge resting on his waist. In his other hand, which he kept raised in an affected manner, he held a cigarette, which he puffed, occasionally throwing his head back in an exaggerated motion. Ordinarily Camila would have been glad to see him, but right then she was disturbed by the way he carried his books, the same way she had carried her books when she had been a schoolgirl. She continued to walk behind him slowly enough to increase the distance between them. At the door, she waited several minutes hoping to give him sufficient time to get on the elevator before she made her entrance. She was relieved to walk into an empty lobby and waited for the elevator to return. When it finally came down, she nodded a perfunctory greeting to those exiting. She got in and pressed five. The elevator stopped at two. There he stood with the books still against his waist.

"Hello, Camila dear, how are you?"

"All right, and yourself?"

"Couldn't be better. That's how life is, you know, one day in the dumps and the next in heaven. Are you sure you're all right? You don't look well. You do have to take care of yourself because, after all, if you don't look out for *numero uno* who will? Listen are you sure you're going to make it to the fifth floor?"

"Thank you, I'm all right," she said.

"Good, good because I wouldn't know what to do if you fainted on me. Is there something wrong? You keep staring at me."

"Oh no, no," she said. "It's just that you look so...so much like someone I remember from back home; Harry, the gardener. He had a very polished look, if you know what I mean?"

"I know exactly. I wasn't born with such a gorgeous face. I have to work at it. Hey, listen, are you all right?"

"I'm okay," she said.

The elevator stopped at five.

"Listen, I'll walk you to your door."

"No, no need. I'm all right."

"Are you sure?"

She stepped out and walked down the corridor. She did not hear the elevator door close. She concluded that Larry was keeping an eye on her to see that she got safely to her door. He was a nice person. Tomorrow she would go up and apologize, though he would have no inkling of what she was apologizing for. Once inside, she leaned up against the wall and waited for the nausea to subside. Some things were best ignored, but memory overwhelmed her.

She saw herself jumping rope in the backyard, counting each time the rope hit the ground. She wanted to outdo Margaret, who lived three houses away and who always bragged about how she jumped longer than everyone else. Camila was determined to do one better; she was determined to go the longest and move the furthest. She started by the side of the porch and moved along to the back end of the house, and turned, the rope still moving. She proceeded back to where she started. She stopped for a minute to catch her breath then began again. This time she would go all the way to the garden shed. Yes, she could do it. She urged herself on until she reached the shed. About to turn, she heard something inside. The usually shut door slightly ajar, she guessed that her father was probably the one in there. She would get him out to marvel at her achievement. Through the slightly open door she saw her father and Harry, their lips touching.

§

Sheldon emerged from the darkness to rub himself against her leg and wake her from her reverie. Walking into the living room, she found Roberto asleep on the couch. "I don't know what I'm going to do about Roberto," she said half to herself and half to Sheldon.

She brought a blanket and covered the sleeping figure.

She then gathered the newspaper that Roberto had dropped on the floor, and intending to look through the real-estate section, she took it into the bedroom with her. Once in bed, she perused the paper for a while. Then she suddenly got up, walked to the dresser and turned the picture of her father face down, so that on getting up in the morning, she would avoid his gaze.

# Dark from the Tap

AROUND 3 O'CLOCK, Mario walked into Harry's Bar. There were only a couple of other guys in the place.

"Dark from the tap," Mario said.

Harry looked up from wiping glasses that had just come up from the kitchen, a few drops of water still on them. "Yeah? You have proof of age?"

"Yeah, I always carry my birth certificate with me," Mario said.

"So, let me see it."

"I'll let you see mine if you let me see yours."

"I'll bet you use that line all the time," Harry said.

"Haven't in a while," Mario said. "That's the sad part of my life."

Harry put the glass under the tap and pulled the lever. The dark liquid flowed until the foam crested over the mouth of the glass. "Here you go," Harry said. "I'll let you slide this time, but next time you do have to show me your birth certificate."

"How about my draft card?" Mario asked.

"Those I don't trust," Harry said, "too many fakes."

"Oh, yeah? I never heard that."

"Maybe you're as young as you look."

"I'm getting old Harry, and all alone too. Women never come into this place."

"Well, that's true, not too many women truck drivers," Harry said, "except your neighbor."

"True, Nancy is a truck driver, and she looks it too. Her partner is something else, though. Does she ever come in here?"

"Not yet," Harry said. "I'm waiting. She'd be good for business."

"Are you planning a change in clientele?"

"Listen kid, she looks all right, and looks is all that counts. These guys who come in here, they won't know the difference. And the ones that already know her, they all think they're men enough to change her ways. They'd be buying the drinks, and the cash register will be ringing."

"Okay, next time I run into her I'll tell her you're looking for help."

"You do that. I'd appreciate it. And who knows, maybe she swings both ways, and she'll be kind to you. Of course, there are those on the fifth-floor. Have you tried them?"

"Harry, I'd have to be really desperate to pay for service."

"You know, kid, you're an idealist. Good to know that there are still kids like you around. But, you're bound to grow-up sooner or later. I can't say whether that's good or bad."

"Well, being alone isn't great right now."

"Hey, things are bound to change for the better, kid. How about another beer?"

"Nah, I've got to get back to work."

"Still writing?"

"Yeah, I'm trying to get ready for a novel."

"For that you'll need a woman around to cook your supper."

"Is that what it is? I thought I needed to experience life a bit more."

"That's one of those false views about art; that it comes from experience. Don't you know that the greatest writers did their best work while they were young? And some of them, their very first book was their best. How do you account for that?"

"Well, maybe you're right, maybe I'll just sit at my desk right now and my best work will just pop out." He pulled out his wallet, and placed some bills on the bar. "I'm off to the mines, then."

"Okay kid; keep your nose to the grindstone."

He walked out to Spring Street and at the corner turned to get to the entrance on Renwick.

Chuck was sitting on the stoop. A taxi had just pulled up to the curb. Two of the girls from the fifth floor got out. The younger one, Sunflower Kelly, turned and leaned into the taxi to speak to someone who wasn't getting out. Her slight bend into the vehicle caused her mini-skirt to raise enough to reveal her undergarment; the color, a majestic purple. Chuck figured the girls must have just made some money and might be ready to spend it on a relaxing commodity. He greeted them as they approached the stoop.

"Hey, ladies, I have some grade 'A' stuff at a bargain price."

"Come up to our place," Alice said. "We'll work something out."

"I only deal in cash," Chuck reminded her.

"In that case, you'll have to see Corky."

"Is that so? Why the hell you let that guy run your business beats me."

"Well, nobody's asking you."

"I don't charge for advice, and when you're ready for the other stuff you know where to find me."

"You sure are talkative today," Sunflower put in.

"For you, honey, the words will flow," Chuck answered.

"We'll make something else flow too, for a slight fee," Alice said.

"That, I can get for nothing," Chuck said.

"Is that so? I don't think you're getting any these days. You look pale and wan."

"I'm not into sun tanning," Chuck assured her.

"Just let me know when you want to restore a little color. You know, make your heart pump and your blood flow." She let out a little laugh and continued up the steps.

Sunflower followed her, and up one landing she turned to check whether Chuck was watching. Men appreciated viewing her from that angle. They often commented on the color of her under-garment. Chuck, however, had not dallied on the stairway, and for a moment, observing the emptiness of the spot where he had been standing, Sunflower felt abandoned.

§

Back in his apartment, Chuck stood in front of the mirror and examined his face. He wondered whether Alice was right, whether deprivation showed on his face, or whether she was trying to trick him into having her way and get around his better judgment.

He did need a woman. Sally had suddenly left. She had just said, "I'm ready to move on," and she had packed up and walked out. She hadn't much to pack, just her clothes, a few trinkets and her personal toiletries. She fit everything into a backpack, swung it on her shoulder and took off. She didn't even say where she was going. Of course, he hadn't asked. The shock of her leaving had muzzled him. That often happened to him, his mouth refusing to let the words through, as if they were allergic to saliva and tried to avoid that passage. That was a disability of course, but few people labeled it as such. More often he was blamed for not saying what needed to be said, as if he had weighed the pros and cons and had decided to keep quiet. That wasn't the case at all. The words just didn't come to him until it was too late, until their moment had passed.

Of course, he knew nothing he said would have kept Sally from leaving. He saw the obstinacy in her face; her leaving was not open for debate. But maybe it was not Sally's absence that troubled him but just the absence of somebody. All he needed was the proximity of a body, something he could sense when he entered the place, at night in bed a body next to his. Did it matter whether that body had Sally's long black hair or whether it dressed in long skirts and wore jingle bells around her ankles? He did remember the sound of the bells as Sally walked down the hall and descended the steps never to return.

§

On his way up the stairs, Mario ran into Sunflower sitting on the steps leading to the third floor. Tears had run down her face and streaked her makeup. She held a piece of paper and an envelope lay on the floor between her high heels. Mario looked straight into her eyes, and the plea he saw in them startled him. She usually smirked as if to dismiss him, and he had always complied without protest. She was, after all, a commodity for which he was unwilling to pay, and he often wondered why anybody parted with cash for something available simply for exchange. True, at the moment he had nobody with whom to exchange, but he looked forward to resolving that problem.

Sunflower wasn't about to replace anybody. She merely sat on the stairway apparently attempting to recover from the message on the piece of paper in her hand.

"Couldn't be all that bad," Mario said and grinned to disguise his apprehension about her possible response.

"How would you know?" she said.

"I don't," he admitted.

"I don't suppose your mother was ever nasty to you?"

"Not that I recall," he said.

She stared at him trying to decide whether she should say anything more. He tried to keep his eyes from her bare thighs and shifted his gaze up to her face. She had hazel eyes, her hair a dirty blond. She reminded him of Iris from his childhood back on Rogers Place, and he wondered whether the figure in his memory was somewhere sitting on some stoop crying for some reason which he might never understand, the way he didn't understand the time he had seen her walking with Cano, the ex-con. He was the last person in the world Mario would have imagined Iris falling for, Iris who attended Catholic school rather than traipsing with the rest of the Rogers Place gang to PS 99 on Stebbins Avenue.

"Tomorrow is always better than today," Mario said.

"Says who?" Sunflower retorted.

"Me, of course," he replied.

He wondered whether he was speaking the truth. He had to, he told himself. He had to, but he remembered a time when he had been ready to give up on that belief, when it just didn't happen, when day after day there seemed to be no way out of the darkness that enveloped him. Somehow those days had come to an end, but now he could not recall what had happened, what had caused the darkness to recede. It had been a night that had lasted several years, but the sun had eventually risen.

He wondered now whether Sunflower was undergoing a similar experience. Of course, he wasn't sure that what he had gone through was universal, that all young people experience it, that it was the same as what Sunflower was currently undergoing.

"I sent my mother a birthday card," she said.

"Ah, and she responded with a letter."

"No, she tore it up without opening it."

"How do you know that?" he asked, though the answer was quite visible. "Someone could be putting you on," he said. "You never know about these things."

Her face revealed her weighing of that option, the process rather short, automatic, and beyond conscious control, like the blinking of an eye. "Oh no, I know it's true," she said. "I know it."

"Do you really?"

She stared at him wishing that he were a wise man revealing to her some truth beyond her power to perceive on her own, that he had looked into the void and had seen an ultimate truth that now he was passing on to her, and she had but to accept it to make everything all right.

"Hey, you want to stop in for some coffee?" The words popped out without his debating whether to say them or not.

They woke her from her stupor. "Nah, why am I talking to you?" she asked and got up.

He watched her walk up to the next landing where she turned to display her annoyance at almost having fallen into the trap, as if she were a child, and he was inviting her into his mother's bedroom.

He was about to raise his arm in a gesture of farewell, but the invisible weight of futility held it down. "See you," he faintly said.

# Reader and Adviser

*I* *WAS ALWAYS NERVOUS* with girls, always scared that I would say the wrong thing or do something stupid, and they would make fun of me. So most of the time, when I was with them I couldn't find nothing to say that sounded smart. When we was kids, my cousin Silvia and me we used to go to the movies together. We used to go to the Loews on Prospect Avenue. On Saturdays, we saw three features for only fifty cents. We used to hold hands and pretend that we was girlfriend and boyfriend, but when we got a little older, she didn't want to do that no more. I thought that she was getting to be like the other girls, the ones that wasn't my family. I didn't want that to happen, 'cause then it would be hard to talk to her and be with her. It was happening, and I was sorry, but I didn't know what to do about it.

Silvia was always nice to me. I felt okay with her, but she was my cousin, you see, and that meant that I shouldn't be thinking the things I was thinking about her. Charlie Soto said that he had been with Iris Rivera behind the stairs in her building, you know where the mailboxes are, and he put his hand up her skirt. I thought maybe that was true. Then again maybe it wasn't, 'cause even if she did like him, why would she let him do that? That was a puzzle to me. Anyway, I couldn't be doing anything like that with Silvia on account of she was my cousin. I didn't want to do nothing that would make her think I didn't respect her. My mother always said that men should respect women, and I think that's right. So if I got Silvia alone somewhere, and I started to feel her up, I thought that maybe she would think that I wasn't respecting her.

One day I was over at Silvia's pretending that I needed help with my homework. We was sitting really close together. Her mother had gone next door to talk to the neighbor. Silvia's leg rubbed against mine. I couldn't stop thinking about how fluffy her body must be under her clothes. The smell of her was driving me crazy.

"Carlito, you're not listening," she said.

"I am, I am," I said. "Keep going. I'm getting it now."

"No, you're not," she said. "What's the matter with you? You're so jumpy!"

"Arithmetic always makes me nervous," I said.

"I think you're lying. I think there's something else on your mind."

"I don't know what that could be," I said.

"I don't know what it could be either," she answered. After a pause she said, "You remember when we was children, and we used to take showers together?"

I had tried to forget that, be'cause I thought she would be embarrassed, if she thought that I remembered. It was something I was never gonna talk about, and there she was throwing it right in my face.

"Yeah, I remember," I said at last. My ears was burning. I figured my face must've been all red, and that made me all the more uneasy, 'cause I didn't want her to see that I was embarrassed. I took my books to leave. "I better go," I said.

"Running away?" she asked. "I'm not going to bite you, you know."

I left as fast as I could. Later I told my friend André what happened. He said I threw away a great opportunity. But that's easy to say if you wasn't there, if you wasn't the one involved. 'cause what was I supposed to do? Make out with my cousin right there in her own house? What if my aunt walked in on us? What then? And anyway I wasn't even sure that Silvia wanted to make out with me. I mean, she could've just been curious to know if I remembered about us taking showers together. We was only little kids when that happened.

On my way home from school one day, I was feeling so miserable that I decided to go into St. Anthony's and pray for a miracle. I knew that it was a sin to think that way about Silvia, so maybe if I prayed the saints would help me to fall out of love with her, or maybe to love her in a less painful way, if that was possible. I don't know why I thought I would get help from the saints on this one. I had never got no help before on anything that was important, like on not failing a test in school or nothing like that. The saints was batting a low average in my league, but I was desperate.

On the left altar there was a statue of St. Joseph, and on the right was the Virgin Mary. I went to the left, 'cause I figured Joseph could understand my problem better than Mary, and anyway I didn't wanna be talking that kind of language in front of a virgin. I knelt down in front of the offering candles, and I lit one. I dropped a nickel in the box before I started to pray. Then I went right ahead and told Joseph my whole problem. I'm sure he knew it already. I'm sure he knew it the minute I stepped into the church. But it was part of what you had to do when you prayed to a saint. You had to tell'm your problem, even though he knew it already. I told'm everything. Then I said, "I know you can help me, 'cause you must've had the same problem with Mary, and I know you licked it. Unless you and Mary put one over on us, you know how to solve this problem, so don't let me down, please." Then I said an Act of Contrition and three Hail Mary's to top it off.

I sat down in one of the pews to wait and see if anything would happen right away. I got to looking at the stained glass windows, 'cause I hadn't been to church in a long time, and I always liked to look at the windows. All them colors was so pretty. That was the only good thing about going to church. When I was a kid I could've died of being bored every Sunday when I went to Mass, except that I got into looking at all the colors and shapes that made up the pictures on the windows. While I was sitting there waiting for Saint Joseph's help to arrive, Father Alfonso walked out of the vestry. I put my head down fast, pretended to be praying like crazy, but it was too late. He'd seen me.

"Is that you Carlito Torres?" he said, narrowing his eyes. "I haven't seen you here in ages, especially at this hour of the day. What's wrong?"

"No problem. I just came to pray."

"Well, you come right over here for confession, and I want to see you at communion on Sunday."

Father Alfonso was a confession freak. Every time he seen you, he wanted you to confess. That's why when I saw him, I was wishing he wouldn't see me, but he came right over to where I was sitting. He had a round puffy face. He looked like an owl, maybe 'cause his eyes was so big and his nose and mouth so small. He was short too, almost a midget. His face was funny, but he had a good voice for preaching. On Holy Week, people came from other parishes to hear him, especially women. But my favorite sermon was the one when he told about how he got his calling. See, he used to be a sailor, and he was in a shipwreck. You should've heard him tell about the wreck; how the wind was howling and how the waves was like mountains crashing down on the ship. Then he was floating on the sea for days. He was just holding on to some wreckage. He thought he was gonna die, but he got this idea. See, he decided to make a bargain with God. He said, "God, if you get me out of this one, I promise to be a priest for as long as you want." Well, low and behold, he gets rescued. A miracle, he says. God must've been hard up for priests. That's what I think. Anyway, it's a good story. I could listen to it over and over, 'cause the way he tells it makes you feel like you're right there, like you was watching a movie of it.

I followed him to the confessional. I told him everything I could think of that I did wrong, but I didn't tell him what I was thinking about Silvia. That was my only big sin, 'cause I hadn't been the one who killed the cat in the empty lot on Intervale Avenue. That was Hector, and he tried to blame it on me. I did throw a rock at the cat, but I missed. So I didn't tell Father Alfonso about the cat, though maybe I should've told him that I was there when it happened. I told'm about the fist fight with Raymond Cazario, but that wasn't such a big sin either, 'cause it was Raymond's fault, and he should confess it and not me. It wasn't a real confession unless I told him about Silvia, but I couldn't bring myself to do it, so I only said I had unclean thoughts about girls. He said not to worry about it; it was only natural.

The penance was five Hail Mary's, but since I had already said three Hail Mary's when I was praying to Saint Joseph, I figured I only had to say two more. I did that and left. I wasn't long out of the church, when I began to suspect that Saint Joseph wasn't into helping me. My suffering over Silvia was just the same as before. Maybe it would take a few days for help to get to me, I said to myself. Maybe Saint Joseph was busy with some other matter just then.

§

Teresina was a friend of my mother's. Well, she wasn't exactly a friend. She lived across the street, and she had a kid, who my mother took care of sometimes when Teresina could find a job. Teresina wasn't young, but she wasn't that old. She couldn't have been more than nineteen, I think. She always used to tease me when she saw me, and I didn't mind 'cause she never teased me about nothing I really cared about, like some people did, especially my uncles. Teresina was a little plump, if you know what I mean. Her hair was always different. She was really a brunette, but sometimes she was a blond and sometimes a red head, and she always wore very red lipstick on her mouth that looked like it had been cut out of a magazine and pasted on her face. Still, it was a very pretty face with a small nose.

Getting together with Teresina wasn't my idea. I could've never thought of it, 'cause she was older than me, was married and had a kid. It wasn't like she could be my regular girlfriend, and like I said she was kind of chubby, though I didn't mind that so much. I guess she felt sorry for me, 'cause she saw me moping around. She didn't know that it was on account of Silvia, but maybe she figured that it was something like that, 'cause when she came to pick up her kid she teased me about what a Casanova I must be. Anyway, I didn't pay no mind to what she said. I had other things to think about. You see, André gave me this idea. He said I should forget about Silvia, and if I wanted some sex I should go to a pro.

"A ho?"

"Yeah, why not? It's just for practice. Then you'll know what to do with regular girls."

"Did you ever go?" I asked him.

"Nah, but I didn't need no practice. Some people just got talent, know what I mean? But some people like to practice. Like my cousin Ricardo, he says he practices on pros all the time, then he can go home and be an expert with his wife."

"I don't think I can do it," I said. "Besides, I don't know any pros."

"The Gypsies," he said, "the ones over the barbershop."

"They just read cards," I said. I had heard that those Gypsies did it, but how was I to know if that was true or not. "Anyway I don't have no money," I said to André.

"They have different prices. You can ask for the five dollar one."

"What could you get for five dollars? An ugly one?"

"What do you care? It's just for practice."

"Where am I gonna get five dollars anyway?"

"What about that can of money you have?"

He was talking about my piggy bank, a used up can of tomato sauce with a slit on top. I used to drop my change in there. I was saving for something special. I don't know what. Maybe I just wanted to have a whole lot of coins to spend all at once, when the can was full.

"I don't think there's five dollars in there yet."

"Check it out, see how much you have."

So André came home with me, and we opened up the can. There was only three dollars and twelve cents in there.

"Not enough," I said.

"All you need is two more dollars."

"It might as well be a hundred. I don't see how I can get no two dollars."

"I have two dollars," he said.

I looked at him right in the eyes. I didn't believe he was gonna give me no two dollars, and I was right. He wanted to buy my knife. You see, I had this boss jack-knife that I had found in Fort Tryon Park, over in Manhattan. This knife had all kinds of thingamajigs on it, a corkscrew, a can opener, a spoon, a screwdriver, even a pair of scissors. Can you dig that? Scissors! I caught on to him right away.

"You're trying to gyp me," I said. "That knife is worth more than two dollars."

"Gyp you? You didn't pay nothing for that knife. You're making a profit on it. You don't have to sell it, you know. If you think I'm trying to gyp you, don't sell it."

I finally sold him the knife, even though I knew it was worth more than two lousy dollars.

I had the five dollars, but it didn't do me no good 'cause I was chicken. I walked up and down the block, but every time I walked in front of the Gypsy shop my feet wouldn't turn to go up the stairs. The Gypsies was right over the barbershop, which was a little below ground level. To get a haircut you had to walk down a few steps, but to get screwed you had to walk up the stoop. André was watching from the corner, so about the tenth time I passed in front of that house I finally started up the steps. I felt like there was some alley cats fighting in my stomach.

Just then I heard Teresina's voice calling out to me. "Hey, Carlito, what are you doing there? You gonna have your palm read?" She winked at me when she said that.

I was so embarrassed I could only smile at her like a fool. I had been so worried about going up those steps that I hadn't noticed her walking down the block, carrying two bags of groceries.

"Help me with these," she said.

So I had to do it, "cause what could I say? I can't help you now Teresina; I gotta go up there and get laid?

"If you want your fortune told, I could do that for you," she said.

I made like I really was interested in knowing the future. "Can you really do that?"

"Sure I can," she said. "I'm part Gypsy myself. I can read cards like a pro."

"That's *chévere*," I said. "You know my grandmother used to read cards too." I wasn't sure if that was true or not. I sort of made it up. Though it could've been true. I don't mind making things up that could've been true. That's not like telling a lie exactly. I took the package all the way to her apartment on the third floor, and she asked me to come in; her kid wasn't there. I figured he must've been with my mother. I put the package on the kitchen table. She offered me a soda, and I sat down to drink it. She took one for herself, and she pulled up one of the chairs, so that she was close enough to touch me with her knees.

"Tell me the real reason why you was going to see them Gypsies," she said.

"I told you already. I wanted them to tell my fortune."

She didn't believe me. "I know better, Carlito, so tell me the truth."

"That's the honest truth, so help me God," I said.

"Don't be sacrilegious," she said. She took my hand. "I have a real good way to read fortunes."

I thought she was gonna read my palm, but instead she put my hand on one of her tits.

"Can you see your future?" she asked. She looked like she was gonna burst out laughing.

"You're making fun of me," I said, taking my hand away from her.

"No, really, I'm not," she said. "Come on."

She took me by the hand again and led me to the bedroom.

"Here, help me with this zipper," she said. She turned around, and I pulled down the zipper of her top. She then pulled it off over her head. My knees had begun to knock together. I didn't know whether I was going to be able to stand at all. I felt sort of helpless confronted with all that flesh. I sat on the bed and watched her.

"Carlito, don't just sit there," she said.

"What should I do?" I stammered. I was glad Teresina was the only one there to hear me say such a stupid thing. Really, what I didn't know was whether I should start undressing myself, or whether I should be helping her take the rest of her clothes off. It seemed like a terrifically important decision to make, but I couldn't make it.

"You can start by taking off your shoes," Teresina said.

Well, once I had started with my shoes, I figured I might as well take everything else off too, so I did. There I was naked as a jaybird. When I looked up, I expected Teresina to be completely bare also, but she was still wearing her bra and her panties. Was I supposed to be naked while she was still covered? Was I doing things the way I was supposed to? I got nervous.

"I left these on for you to help me with," she said. She sat down next to me, and put her arms around me. I fumbled with the snap of her bra, but it wouldn't open. I felt like an idiot. When she noticed that I was more interested in undoing the bra than in anything else, she turned around, so that I could see what I was doing.

It was a great relief to me when she was finally all naked. I had gotten through the first part without any great disaster. But now, like summertime flies in a fruit market, other problems came buzzing by. The first, that I didn't know how long I was supposed to be pumping her. That may sound stupid, but not really. You see, I could've gone on for hours 'cause I could come over and over as many times as she wanted. So, I wasn't sure if I was supposed to know, somehow, when Teresina had enough, or if she was supposed to let me know. She kept moaning and biting and digging her nails into my back, so I figured everything was all right, but I wasn't sure. After I had come three times it struck me that Teresina might get pregnant.

"Teresina," I said almost without wanting to.

"What my darling, *querido*?" she panted back between bites.

"What if you get pregnant?"

"Don't be silly," she said, and she dug her nails into me.

Well, she must know what she doing, I figured, and I buried my face between her tits. At that point I thought I heard someone at the door. Perhaps Teresina's husband was home early. He was a mechanic at a gas station. I could just see him, in his greasy overalls, holding a big iron wrench in his hand. I wouldn't stand a chance.

"Teresina," I said.

"What?" she breathed.

"I think there's somebody at the door."

"It's your imagination," she whispered. "Just a little bit more, don't stop."

I pumped her for all she was worth; she threw her legs up around me and let out a scream. My heart almost stopped. I was sure whoever was at the door had heard.

"Oh, Carlito you're so good," she said.

"I'm glad you think so," I said, waiting for her husband to walk in and bash me on the head with the wrench. He didn't show his face. Her scream must have scared him away.

We got out of bed and got dressed.

"You have talent, Carlito; I knew you had it in you."

"Yeah?" I was surprised at her prophetic powers. "How'd you know?"

"A woman can tell," she said. "With a little practice you'll be A-number-one."

"No kidding?"

"Yeap," she said. "Only one thing, Carlito, you can't tell anybody about this."

"I ain't gonna tell," I said.

"You better not. If my husband finds out he'll kill you."

"That's what I thought."

"Good," she said.

When I got downstairs André was sitting on the stoop waiting for me.

"What took you so long?"

"She wanted me to move some furniture."

"All that time?"

"She couldn't make up her mind where she wanted to put it, so we kept moving it from place to place."

"You can go back to the Gypsies now," he said.

"I don't think I want to," I said. "I want to buy my knife back."

He was surprised and very reluctant, but finally he gave it back to me, and I gave him his two dollars.

§

Even though it was Silvia I really wanted, me and Teresina we got it together every chance we got. Sometimes I pretended that it was Silvia I was holding instead of Teresina. That way it was like making love to both of them. One thing about Teresina, though, she would do it anywhere. And I mean anywhere! We did it on a kitchen table once. I was on the bottom that time. Would you believe the bathroom at P.S. 99? That's right, on parent's night. She went in to see her cousin's teachers in place of her aunt. I went with Teresina be'cause she didn't want to have to walk home alone. I don't know why the hell her husband didn't take her. That time we did it sitting down. Then there was the time in Don Justino's grocery store. Teresina was minding the store. When I walked in, just to buy some licorice, she locked the door and pulled me to the back. We did it right there on the floor, lying between sacks of potatoes and onions. I can still remember the smell of the onions. The German shepherd that Don Justino kept for protection, chained to the butcher block, kept growling the whole time.

While I was sneaking around getting my share of Teresina, Silvia got herself knocked up. They made her get married, even though she was only fourteen. She had a regular wedding and everything. She asked me to be an usher, but I said I couldn't do it. I guess maybe I should have, so as not to hurt her feelings, but I don't like to be in the spotlight—you know, get photographed and walk down the aisle and things like that, with lots of people looking on. Everyone was nice to Silvia, so as not to hurt her feelings. Everyone pretended like it was a normal kind of wedding and not the sort that had to be. All the relatives acted like they was having a good time. I think part of why they was having such a good time was that now they could say something nasty about Silvia behind her back. That's the way those people are, two-faced. If they can say something nasty about you, they feel good 'cause then they think they're better than you.

Silvia looked terrific in her white dress. With the veil over her face nobody could tell, as she walked up the aisle, that she was crying. Even tear-stained she looked beautiful when she came out of the church. The groom, too, was handsome. I tried to imagine what kind of a rat he must be, but it was my duty to wish only well on Silvia, and so I was forced to think of him as maybe a nice guy. After all, he was marrying her.

Father Alfonso performed the ceremony, and he also came to the reception in the evening. I was sure glad I hadn't told him in confession how I felt about Silvia. Teresina and her husband were there too. The husband was a quiet sort of a guy, the opposite of Teresina. She danced almost every number, like she would never run out of energy. He sat and talked most of the night, chain smoking little cigars. He drank but not too much. They made a good couple. Everyone said they were very happy together.

# Joanie

*T*HE LANDSCAPE FLITTED by like the frames of a silent movie. Vast wheat fields undulated with the wind like an ocean of yellow waves. In the distance, a giant harvester resembled a ship steaming from one continent to another. Above the field a blue sky extended replete with silver clouds intent on playing games of transformation as they tried to disguise themselves by taking the shapes of mythological beasts. Joanie had boarded in Illinois, and the seat next to her remained empty until the bus reached Indianapolis, where a middle-aged man got on and sat next to her.

Perhaps in his mid-forties or early fifties, the hair above his ears graying, he reminded her of her father. It was the middle of the day, and no doubt her father was at work in the factory where he operated a milling machine. She recalled how sometimes he referred to it fondly and other times described it as the curse of his life. When sober, he was reasonable enough and considered time at work a part of life everyone had to deal with. He often claimed that he was lucky to be attached to that machine as if it were part of his body like another set of arms and legs or an extension of his natural ones. When he drank, a different story emerged, like a cork that had been tied to some stone at the bottom of a pond and somehow had been let loose, the bind accidentally cut, gnawed by some creature of the deep with sharp teeth and intent on causing havoc, or with no intention at all but merely a natural impulse with consequences irrelevant to its survival.

The man took out a newspaper from his attaché case and perused the headlines. She glanced sideways from the corner of her eye to catch the word "Saigon." Perhaps she would have been better off going there rather than to New York, though that had not been her intention when she enlisted. She had been fleeing from home. Of course, that didn't necessarily require joining up. It had been a spur of the moment decision, if there was ever such a thing. The recruiter had first approached her as she crossed the parking lot of the supermarket where she worked as a cashier. She had just gone through hours of boredom, and she was annoyed at having to go through register check. At the end of the shift, the money in the register had to match the sum on the machine's automatic tally. If it came up short, the difference was deducted from her pay, but when the opposite happened she didn't get to keep the difference. She had already lost money several times.

The recruiter had a cheerful smile on his face.

"You have a minute?" he asked. "It may change your life for the better."

"Oh, yeah?"

"Just listen, then you can decide," he said.

"I haven't got time right now," she responded and walked on.

Perhaps something in her voice told the man that she wasn't completely rejecting his suggestion. He saw a prospect, and he again approached her the next day. Four months had elapsed since then.

He had convinced her, or rather, it appeared that his

persuasion had tipped the balance, had moved her to sign the papers and head off to training camp. She didn't know what really moved her or what she was searching for. Perhaps she was trying to escape from fetters that she felt but only vaguely recognized. She could not say where the urge came from or where it was taking her. She had looked at her mother and had retrieved an image from long before. She remembered her mother's smile, the one that had gradually disappeared over the years. Submerged by some mysterious aura that had gradually seeped into her body, it had eventually paralyzed the muscles of her face so that the smile became a rare occurrence. Perhaps it was then that Joanie began to suspect that the same ailment might afflict her, like a virus that attacked the eyes causing the inability to see colors, the world becoming a miasma of grey tones, some darker than others but brightness completely absent. Why would her mother have abandoned her smile if she could still see the colors of the rainbow? Why not leave this place that might take away the urge to smile? The recruiter offered her a chance to get away, a secure job for few years. She would get paid to take a trip away from the slums of Chicago. There were other places to explore.

When she got home, the image of the recruiter popped up, and she was force to scrutinize it. Something about the good-looking guy in the uniform was different from the usual. His body conveyed a message, assured her that he knew what he was talking about. His image symbolized what a man should be, what she suspected her father had once been. There was no way to be sure of that, but she felt it. She didn't have to think about it, just like she didn't have to think about breathing or adjusting her eyes to deal with the light that at any moment enveloped her. When the recruiter approached her the next day, she didn't really listen to what he had to say. She had already made up her mind. She signed up.

Her father's reaction was less severe than she expected. "They're going to make you earn your keep, and you better do it right and keep out of trouble. The military is a guy's world and you better keep that in mind. Stay out of trouble. You hear me?"

"Of course, I hear you. Even the neighbors can hear you."

What kind of trouble did he think she could get into? She had dropped out of school, but that wasn't trouble. She just didn't want to sit there listening to all that nonsense, about history and science, and when would she ever have to solve an equation?

"Are you sure you want to do this?" her mother asked.

"Better than just hanging out here." Indeed, that's what she felt. She would be off to see the world and have a good time.

"It won't be easy," her mother said.

"And your life here—is that easy?"

Her mother kept quiet and merely looked down as if the formulation of an answer would pop up from the cracked linoleum tile of the kitchen floor.

"I'll be all right," Joanie said.

She wasn't all right for long, and now she was on her way to New York, because she had to go somewhere, and she was certain that she wouldn't be welcomed home.

At the Port Authority bus terminal, Joanie descended the bus steps to be assailed by the smell of oil and gasoline released by the giant vehicles that dominated the space like prehistoric beasts emitting their foul waste as they rested. She waited for her valise to be retrieved from the storage compartment in the bowels of the creature, and once in hand, she proceeded to the steps and up to the main lobby of the terminal. She had no idea what to do next. She had never before been in New York, and she didn't know exactly in what direction to head.

She had heard about the Lower East Side, a place where hippies hung out. She would be welcomed there no doubt, even though she didn't consider herself one of them. She wasn't rejecting the ordinary everyday life. She had been a soldier after all, even if only for a short time. She hadn't chosen to leave. She had been asked to leave, or rather, had been ordered to leave; she had been discharged. Through no fault of her own, she had gotten into trouble. Well, maybe she was partially to blame. She couldn't deny responsibility, but she had not intended for things to go that far.

The attendant at the information booth, a short wiry man for so sedentary a job, smiled as she approached. She could tell that her looks had an effect on him. She asked for directions to the East Village.

"Take the 'A' train down to Fourteenth Street," he said. "Then the shuttle across to Union Square. From there, the IRT will take you as far down as you want to go."

She smiled and thanked him, then headed for the exit.

Out in the street the city assailed her. It was strange to be in new place, somehow both the same and different from what she had imagined it would be. She had grown up in a city. This one wasn't much different. It was just not home. She could tell that she was downtown, and she had to get somewhere that would feel more hospitable. It was sunny and hot. She walked to Eighth Avenue and descended into the subway. She followed the directions and got out at Astor Place.

With no idea of what to do next, she randomly chose a direction and strolled until she got to a street closed to traffic. She proceeded halfway down the block and sat down on a stoop to watch the children play under a fire hydrant sprinkler. She considered slipping out of her sandals and joining them. No doubt the water would be soothing, and her feet would get some relief, but she just sat there contemplating the scene.

An older woman approached her and informed her that she couldn't hang out on the block.

"I'm just sitting here. What's that to you?"

"This block is cordoned off for day camp activities. It's not a hangout for strangers."

"I've nowhere to go," Joanie said.

One of the street workers came over. She was a young woman, her features very severe, her body rather angular, implying that physical closeness might result in bruises.

"You're not from around here, are you?" the young woman said.

"Just got here."

"Where are you headed?"

"I have no place to go," Joanie responded. "You know any where I can put up for the night?"

Merrill, the wiry young woman, mulled that over. "Let's see what we can do," she said at last, and went off to speak to her supervisor.

The next day, Joanie and Harry emerged from the subway at Spring Street and walked west toward the river. On either side of the street, trucks were being loaded or unloaded. Some had pulled right up to the elevated loading zones and blocked the sidewalk, so pedestrians had to walk around them on the cobble-stoned street. As they crossed Van Dyke, Harry said, "I think it's the next block." When Merrill had called early that morning while they were still having breakfast, he had written down the address on his note-pad.

Joanie had spent the night at Harry's, or rather at his parent's apartment. For the summer, he was home from school and working in the street program. Merrill had canvassed her friends to find Joanie a place to stay for a few days. Someone agreed to put her up, and Harry was taking her there now. Joanie figured that she would have a respite while she looked for a job and arranged for something more permanent.

Harry had offered to carry her valise, a small one with not much in it. She could handle it herself, but she let him carry it to make him feel better. He needed reassurance just then. He had yet to recover from the previous evening. She had merely been trying to thank him for offering to put her up for the night. He was a very pleasant boy, and she had no idea what kind of person she would encounter the next day. He would probably be nice, too. Why else would he have agreed to take her in? He was a friend of these people, of Merrill and Isabel anyway. Isabel had dropped by; no doubt to make sure that she wasn't foisting an unacceptable person on her friend.

"That must be the place, on the corner," Harry said.

She gazed across the street at the five-story building. A

bar occupied the street level floor, its entrance on Spring Street. Access to the apartments was around the corner on the wide side of the building that faced Renwick Street. Age had darkened the century-old yellow bricks of the structure, the fight against time a futile battle.

"This neighborhood isn't that residential," Harry said.

"Looks fine to me," Joanie responded.

She made a gargantuan effort to maintain high spirits. For his part, Harry had never met anyone like her, and he regretted passing her on to someone else. But simultaneously, he felt relieved.

At forty-seven Renwick Street, they proceeded up the stairs to Mario's apartment on the third floor. The young man ushered them in. Harry introduced himself, put down the valise, and then introduced Joanie. The host scrutinized Joanie very intently, as if he was examining a delivery object, and it wasn't exactly what he had ordered.

Sounding reluctant, but something within urging him to exit before an unforeseen problem materialized, Harry said, "Well, I have to get to work." He followed by extending his hand to Mario, who still looked perplexed. After a slight bow to Joanie, Harry made his exit, relieved to hear the door shut and bolted behind him.

§

So here she was at Mario's place. She looked around and saw that it was rather Spartan. Men were like that she figured, no frills, content with the bare necessities. It was a woman's job to help them out. She would do that, repay him for his kindness. Nevertheless, a question lurked in the underbrush of her consciousness. If he was used to living alone, would he bear having someone else around? Then, there was Isabel to consider. Joanie had sensed something when she met her. Isabel had been friendly; there was kindness in her face. But there was something else there, too; a spark of fear behind the knowledgeable eyes, and behind the smile, a doubt about sending her over to Mario's place.

She refrained from asking Isabel about her concern. Better not to stir the pot and bring up something that should just as well remain at the bottom. If Mario was Isabel's man, that was all right. She wasn't looking for a man. A man had gotten her into trouble. She just needed a place to stay, a place to sleep for a few nights. She wouldn't be staying long. She would get her own place as soon as she got a job. In the meantime, she would just be nice to Mario and help him out, keep house for him. He would appreciate that. He seemed a nice enough guy. She would be straightforward with him. After all, she really didn't have anything to hide, and her condition would become obvious soon enough.

"Boy, this place could use some curtains," she said. "I'll make some for you."

A look of panic undulated over Mario's face. His fear emerged like a trapped animal suddenly springing from an opened cage. "I like it the way it is," he snapped.

She had said the wrong thing. She was just offering to do something for him, make the place a little more homelike, gentler, less like an army barrack. She had just left that environment. She had put up with it for a reason, but nothing was forcing Mario to do that, except that he was a man. He needed a woman's touch to make the place more cheerful. She could provide that for him, just as a thank you. That's all. She didn't intend to take over.

She observed the tension gradually flow out of him, as he read the apology on her face.

"Harry seemed a little put out," Mario said, for his part, trying to steer attention away from him.

"He's been acting a bit funny since this morning," she responded. "I think he felt guilty about going to bed with me."

Mario's puzzled look disconcerted her. Perhaps she was revealing more than he wanted to know. Perhaps he was more innocent than his surroundings claimed. Perhaps, they all were, Merrill and Isabel and Harry, and now Mario. She had stumbled into this different world, not what she had expected in New York.

"At his mother's, he didn't want do anything against the rules," she tried to explain. She wondered how much more she should tell him, whether she could explain why that previous night was irrelevant. She was just trying to be nice, trying to thank Harry for his help, to show him that she was grateful.

"Mothers do have prerogative," Mario said, his tone suggesting that mothers were special, that he loved his own, and the feeling overflowed to include all the others.

"I hope so," she said. "I'm going to be one."

"That's a pretty aspiration."

"Well, I don't really want to be one yet, but what's done is done." His blank look pushed her to elaborate. "I'm pregnant," she said. "That's why I'm here."

"In New York, you mean?"

What did he want to know, whether she had arrived at his place looking for a pregnancy domicile? Thoroughly perplexed, he looked at her as if he were trying to discern some further evidence of her condition.

She looked around the place. One room contained a bed and a dresser, all the drawers empty. "This is the spare room," he said. "It's all yours." She carried the valise into the room and placed it by the bed. She refrained from unpacking. The task required hurdling an emotional barrier, a feat she was yet uncertain of being able to handle. She had to get used to the place. She returned to the kitchen and forced her face into a smile. Mario then pointed to the next room that served as his bedroom as well as his study; a bed and a desk were the only furnishings there.

"Let me show you the neighborhood," he said after she had settled in.

They walked down Spring to Varick, then up Downing to the intersection of Bleecker and Sixth. He pointed out the essential places, the Laundromat, the supermarket, the fruit store, and the pastry shop. They walked up McDougal past The Figaro nightclub. He pointed out The Feenjon, the best falafel place in town. Across the street, her eyes found one jewelry shop after another, each window replete with costume jewelry as well as fancier things. At the corner of Eighth, Fred Leighton's had Mexican lace dresses in the window. Everything fascinated her. She had never before been to a place like this. It all seemed like magic.

"I never expected this," she said. "It was just too awful at home. I had to get away, so I joined the army. I thought I'd have a chance in the military. Get some training in something, you know, then get a job when I got out. But right away I ruined everything. The first time going all the way, I got pregnant. It wasn't any fun either. He was rough on me."

She thought back to the incident that had started out as just a date. They would go see a movie then stop for a drink at one of the local bars that catered to enlistees. Harvey was very tall. She wasn't crazy about his looks, though most women would have been pleased enough. He had that build idealized in the movies, sort of a John Wayne swagger, except that he lacked the promise of understanding that always flowed from the screen images. She was more prone to the vulnerable ones like James Dean. But right then she didn't have much choice. "Some of us are going into town this weekend," Anne Kelly had said. "Want to go with us? We can fix you up with a guy, one of Jack's friends. Anyway, what's the difference, take in a movie and have a drink, that's all." Just a night in town, nothing more, but then one thing led to another. At the bar, he kept buying her drinks, ones she had never had before. She was just used to beer and straight liquor once in a while. This time she fell in love with the whisky sour, and Harvey kept ordering one more. The drink removed the word "no" from her vocabulary.

"That was the worst night of my life," she said to Mario. "When I missed my period two months in a row, I went to the infirmary and that was it. I was discharged. I had nowhere to go, not home, for sure. My father would kill me. Yeah, he would. So I came to New York. There had to be something for me here. So here I am."

"Yes, so here you are," he said.

At the moment, she had not much to lose. In fact, she had nothing at all. The worst that could happen had already occurred, and she was surviving. Out in the streets of an unfamiliar city, she had found shelter the very first day. She didn't have to spend that first night under some stoop in constant fear of having to fend off some deranged drunkard. Here she was with this guy whose look was difficult to decipher but who was willing to take in a complete stranger. He was being kind to her, guiding her through Greenwich Village as if she were a tourist on vacation rather than a homeless person.

That evening, he cooked supper, and she washed the dishes. At bedtime he said, "Well, you have a room all to yourself. You can lock the door if you want to."

"Why would I want to do that?"

"I'm just telling you," he said. "In case you're concerned about it."

She giggled. "You're funny," she said.

He retreated to his desk, and she into the bedroom. She donned her two-piece pink nightgown and returned to the kitchen, brushed her teeth and washed up. Once in bed she called out to him. "Mario, I forgot to turn off the light. Will you do that for me?"

"Sure," he said. "You want me to tuck you in too?"

"Sure do," she answered.

He walked into the bedroom and sat on the side of the bed. He pulled the blanket up to her chin as if he were tucking in a child.

"I have something to ask you," she said.

He stared at her as if he expected some momentous question.

"Are you and Isabel an item?"

"We're just friends," he said. "That's all, nothing romantic. Whatever gave you that idea?"

"Just a feeling I had when she talked about you. I wondered if you two were more than just friends."

"No," he said as he unsuccessfully tried to repress an unpleasant memory.

"It's all right then," she said, raising her hand up to his neck and pulling his face close to hers. "It's all right," she repeated. "Get in here with me."

"I'll turn off the light," he said.

"No leave it on," she said. "I want to see you."

After they made love, she smiled and said, "You're so gentle."

They made love again, and then fell asleep.

§

She got a job selling encyclopedias door-to-door, her territory in Connecticut. She would be gone a week at a time. At first, she feared that selling encyclopedias would be too difficult, but soon enough she discovered that she had a knack for it. That first week she worked in Danbury. The group manager reserved motel rooms for the sales team. Joanie shared a room with a colleague, another young woman. In the morning, the group went out to breakfast, then each was assigned an area to cover. At lunchtime, they were picked up by the supervisor and taken to a luncheonette. Then, they went back to cover another section of town during the afternoon. This went on for the five working days of the week; then back to New York till the next excursion.

She missed Mario while she was away. It was only a week, but on that first night she missed his body next to hers. She looked forward to Friday night when she would be back at Renwick Street. In the evening, when she had time to reflect, she wondered whether he missed her and was thinking of her, but she refrained from calling him. He would be upset with her for wasting money on an unnecessary call. They would just have a good time together when she got home. She missed the place, and she missed him, as if they had been partners for years rather than weeks. When she got back that Friday night, she sensed that he was glad to see her. "You missed me, didn't you?" she said. He didn't answer in words, but merely looked at her sheepishly unwilling to admit what he felt.

On Saturday morning, they went out for breakfast then roamed the streets of the Village as if they were both seeing them for the first time. She wasn't yet showing, and she wondered whether he remembered that she was bearing a child. "You can get an abortion," he had said the day after she had moved in and told him of her condition, the day after she had pulled him into bed with her. It was her last time in that bed because from then on she slept in his bedroom rather than in that extra room. Once, in a fleeting moment, it had occurred to her that one room didn't have to be extra, but she exiled the thought to the realm of improbabilities. She would have to wait for him to arrive at that conclusion. She sensed that making the suggestion would put him in a bind, make him feel trapped into assuming the consequences of someone else's misdoing. She was happy to accept his kindness, but she had to wait for him to take the next step.

§

Returning from a week's work, a stranger at the bus terminal approached her. He sported a yellow bandana around his neck, and on his head, a red hat that would have done credit to d'Artagnan. Tall and thin, though he had no beard, he evoked a dark image of Don Quixote. The bizarre costume, a purple and yellow vest over his ebony skin, and below that, bell-bottom pants to match, caught her eye. The character, who seemed to have just stepped out of the pages of a novel, noticed that she was staring at him.

"I'm Abu," he said making a slight bow. "Can you help me out? I need a place to flop for the night. I just got here with my old lady, but she cut out on me the minute we got off the bus. Now I'm in the pits. All the way from SF, and she dumps me. There's got to be a shelter somewhere around here. Do you know where?"

"I don't know about any shelters. Maybe you should ask an officer."

"A flat foot, you mean, a pig?"

"Sure," she said.

She had a positive view of the New York police. She had once forgotten to take the apartment key, and Mario was out when she got back. She waved down a passing patrol car and explained her predicament.

"Well, let's see what we can do," the first cop said. "What floor are you on?" he asked.

"The third," she told him.

"What do you think, Brian?" the cop said to his partner.

"No problem," Brian said. "We're New York's finest. Aren't we?"

So Officer Brian gave Officer Paul a boost to reach the fire escape ladder and let it down. Then both of them, along with Joanie, climbed up to the third floor landing. The officers forced open the window to let her in. She thanked them profusely before they made their exit through the front door.

Abu had a whole different view of cops, and he wasn't about to go seek their help.

"I really do need a place for the night," he said.

"Well, there's an extra bed in my friend's place," she said before considering what Mario's response might be. He had taken her in. Why not another lost person just for one night?

"This is Abu," she said when Mario opened the door and stared at her and the stranger. Once in the kitchen, she knew that she had made a mistake. "He's got no place to stay," she said in a pleading tone. "And he's hungry."

"I haven't eaten in three days," Abu said.

"There are eggs in the fridge," Mario said.

"I'll scramble some," Joanie offered. From the refrigerator, she pulled out the egg carton and the butter. She retrieved the frying pan from the cabinet by the side of the stove. Abu sat at the table looking more and more like a black version of the scarecrow in *The Wizard of Oz* after having lost a great deal of its straw. Joanie cracked the eggs and scrambled them; she lit the burner then poured the eggs into the sizzling butter in the pan.

"I'm heading back to San Francisco tomorrow morning," Abu explained to Mario. "New York is no place for me. I'm a San Francisco kind of guy. I just need to plop down for the night."

The eggs cooked quickly enough and Joanie poured them on a plate and placed it on the table in front of Abu. She and Mario watched him gobble them down.

Pleadingly Joanie looked at Mario who had not let down his guard. "Can Abu stay, just for tonight?"

"Just for tonight," he said turning to look at Abu. "But you have to cut out in the morning. I'm not running a flophouse."

"That's good enough for me," Abu said. "I'm going to hop a freight back to San Francisco. New York isn't my kind of town."

"You can sleep in there," Mario said pointing to the bedroom he had first offered Joanie. He then retreated to the main room, turned off the light and climbed into bed. Joanie followed him and cuddled up.

"Please don't be angry at me," she said.

"Joanie, you can't do this in New York. It's too dangerous."

"I thought you wouldn't mind," she said. "He had no place to go. You've been so nice to me. I thought you wouldn't mind."

"This guy seems all right, but the next one might not be. You can't do this again."

"All right," she said. She pressed herself up against him and felt his anger dissipate.

§

After breakfast, Abu left like he said he would, in search of the freight yards and a ride home to San Francisco. Mario went off to work, and Joanie began to putter about in the kitchen. After washing the breakfast dishes, she went out for a walk. She ambled down to West Street and up under the highway to the public pier, where she sat down on one of the beams that fenced the edge. She turned her head to look down at the water where sleeks of oil refracted the light to reveal the colors of the rainbow. She thought about Abu. He had done the right thing, had left headed back home. He wasn't a New York person, and neither was she.

The child was on its way and to burden Mario with that problem wasn't fair. Just one time, he had mentioned an abortion, and she pretended to not have heard him. She sensed that he would push for it if he picked up any sign of willingness from her. To take that route would be a greater mistake than the first. She would be guilty of taking a life. This new being was part of her, and she would take care of it as best she could, but she couldn't ask Mario to do that with her. Anyway, Mario was already taken, though he didn't yet know it.

Joanie had sensed right away that Isabel was making a claim, and she watched them pretend to be merely friends. From the beginning, that had been another mistake. Sooner or later Isabel would stop pretending. Then Joanie would have to retreat, not because Isabel had been there first, but because there was no way to dislodge her. Joanie wondered whether she really loved Mario the way Isabel did. She felt that she did, but if so, how could she burden him with a problem that had nothing to do with him. Isabel had been trying to help when she sent her to Mario's place, and now it would be wrong to try to take him away from her.

She walked back to Renwick Street. On her way up the stairs, she saw the old woman who lived in the apartment below. Always on the lookout for something to complain about, she stuck her head out to peek as Joanie went by. "I won't be disturbing you anymore," Joanie said, and continued her climb to Mario's place.

Once in the apartment, she entered the spare room and pulled her small valise from underneath the dresser and placed it on the bed. She retrieved her few items from the dresser drawers and placed them in the valise. She crossed the kitchen into the main room and looked around for anything she might have left there. She spied her comb on

Mario's desk. She picked it up and placed it in her purse. She walked back across the kitchen to the bedroom where her valise still rested on the bed. About to pick it up, she hesitated, debating whether to write Mario a note. No, what good would that do? She would just leave and let him arrive at his own conclusion.

She picked up the valise, walked to the door and out to the hallway. She locked the door then placed the key under the mat. She proceeded to the stairwell and descended out to the street. She turned right on Spring. Tears streaking down her face, she wondered where she was going.

# Rachel or Diane?

*H*AD MARIO BEEN asked for an explanation of why he hung out with Rick, he would have been unable to provide a reasonable answer. Still, there were many sides to a person, and Mario, for the moment, ignored the fact that Rick floated, always high and always ready to provide. Rick had introduced him to Rachel Fitzgerald, but so far that had been of dubious value.

Had he taken a moment to ponder why he was attracted to Rachel, he would have found his conclusions unsettling. Rachel's appeal stemmed from the vagueness of her manner. She possessed a quiet beauty, a quality she attempted to hide, or had no idea existed. She dressed plainly. She had dark hair and fine features, and wearing eyeglasses, she attained an intellectual aura that appealed to him. Her eyeglasses overwhelmed her features. When he looked at her, he felt as if he were the one wearing them, her image magnified.

Meeting her had been another odd occurrence. She had been Rick's friend, but obviously he didn't fit into her conservative leanings, and Mario failed to take that observation a step further to foresee falling into a similar predicament.

"You're not seeing Rachel anymore, are you?" Mario inquired.

"She's not my type," Rick said, then added, "and I don't think she's your type either."

"I beg to disagree."

"Well, you'll find out soon enough," Rick said.

"That's what life's about, isn't it? Exploring the world and finding things out."

"But there's no sense in exploring territory that's already been mapped."

"I don't know about that. People are still climbing the Himalayas."

"And still freezing to death."

"Thanks for the warning."

"Well, what are friends for?"

"So she didn't put out for you, did she?"

"Hey man, you can't win'm all."

"Well, you know, there's more to life than just sex."

"Did I say sex is all?"

"I don't smoke either."

"You must be a poet at heart, and for you, that's almost enough. Still, you've got to have a woman once in a while."

"You have a simple view of life."

"I'm glad you think so, and I wish you were right, but alas, life is too complicated. Let me know how your courtship progresses. I was going to say 'affair,' but it probably won't get that far."

"So you don't mind my stepping in?"

"She's not my wife, is she?"

"That's for sure," Mario said. "So, what attracted you to her in the first place?"

"I guess it's that quiet smile she has behind her spectacles. Of course, that doesn't sound reasonable at all, does it? So maybe there's just something about her that's not obvious. Who knows?"

A week later, Rick asked Mario how his pursuit of Rachel was progressing.

"We went to a poetry reading," Mario said.

"Your idea or hers?"

"Hers," he said disconsolately.

"Let me guess. After the poetry reading, you took her to The Peacock."

The Peacock, on West 4th Street, had period looking tables and chairs that gave the place an antique and foreign look. On the walls hung real paintings in the styles of the Old Masters, though they had been specifically done for the place. The subdued lighting promoted tender feelings.

"I wanted to, but she suggested I take her home," Mario said.

"So she had it with you."

"Well, not quite yet. She invited me up."

"To meet her mother, right?"

"Her mother wasn't home yet. She too was out on a date. I didn't know her parents were divorced."

"A slight detail I forgot to mention."

"Anyway, so I went up to their apartment, a nice place. First she showed me her mother's studio. She's a terrific painter, her mother. Then I sat in the kitchen while Rachel made me a cup of coffee."

"Well, see, she wanted to make sure you didn't fall asleep on her."

"Then we sat in the hammock. Did you know there was a hammock in the living room?"

"Sorry, I never got up to the apartment. You got a lot further than me, though doing it on the hammock doesn't sound too comfortable."

"We just made out. I was touching her all over, and she was about to take off her blouse when her mother came home with her date, and he was drunk. But if I got up, the bulge in my pants would show. So I just sat there for a while until it subsided."

"So, sometimes yours subsides? Mine never does."

"Yeah, right, that's why you didn't get on with Rachel."

"Sure, she was afraid her mother would suspect something was going on."

"Her mother didn't give a damn what was going on. She saw my predicament and had trouble keeping herself from laughing."

"And her boyfriend, did he have a hard-on, too?"

"Shit, the guy was drunk. He could hardly talk, every word slurred. I doubt anything else on him was functioning. He looked like a construction worker, potbelly and all. You never know what women are going for these days."

"Well, so you didn't get everything on the first date. That's normal. Usually doesn't happen on the second date either."

"I may never know."

"So you asked her out again, and she turned you down?"

"I don't know."

"What do you mean, you don't know? Did you ask her out again or not?"

"I did."

"Did she turn you down?"

"She said maybe."

"Well, you can't win'm all, can you?"

"Shit, you have a dark way of looking at everything."

"Not everything. You want some pills?"

Mario gave him a hard look.

"Just kidding. You know I don't push the stuff on my friends."

Rachel became a quandary. Surely flesh and blood, Mario had proof of that now that he had held her close, kissed her, and had been at the point where she seemed willing to undress, if only her mother had not suddenly appeared. But she proceeded to act as distant as before, as if nothing had happened, as if she had not invited him home that night. He began to think that he had imagined the whole incident, or perhaps life was really Kafkaesque. How else could he explain Rachel's strange behavior?

She remained an enigma. Her beauty captivated him, and yet her quietness allowed her to blend into whatever setting she walked into—a chameleon—and perhaps that quality was the attraction that appealed to him. She had blended in with him, but then without warning, without obvious reason, had disappeared. The Rachel he remembered in his arms transformed into someone else, and he remained ignorant of the cause. Indeed, he was ignorant of a great deal; much of the world was invisible to him, or perhaps merely unrecognizable. Rachel's ability to blend in attracted him, but he failed to see how she would merge into whatever milieu surrounded her, and to her, he was replaceable.

§

During the summer, while Rachel was away, Diane approached him, and he went along because most of his acquaintances were away. She had friends in Massachusetts, and she wanted him to meet them. She suggested borrowing his father's car for a trip to Boston to visit her friends.

"We can go by rail," he said.

"It'll be a lot easier if we borrow the car just for the weekend."

"If you want a car, we'll have to rent one," he said.

"I'd rather not spend that much," she said.

On the train they sat across from a woman, on her way to Greenwich, whose gray hair reminded Diane of her mother.

"I come to New York to visit my daughter every other week. I haven't much else to do," the woman said. "My daughter wants me to move to New York, so I don't have to make such a long trip. I tell her I don't mind the trip. It gives me something to do."

"And your husband?" Diane asked.

"Oh, he's gone."

"I'm sorry," Diane said. "When did he pass away?"

"Oh, he's not dead," the woman said after twitching her lips to one side. "He's just gone."

"I'm sorry about that too," Diane said, trying to sympathize.

"I was sorry at first, but now I'm glad. It's a relief not to have to deal with him anymore." After a pause she added, "Every man doesn't turn out to be bad. My daughter's husband is all right. I'm sure yours is, too." She nodded at Mario.

"He certainly is," Diane said, reaching over to Mario who had been on the verge of correcting the woman.

"How long have you been married?"

"Just a few months," Diane said.

"Well, the two of you look like you're doing very well."

The look of success lasted only until the woman got off at Greenwich. Then, Mario revealed his annoyance.

"Why did you say we were married?"

"It seemed like the right thing to say. It's no big deal."

"What's wrong with the truth?"

"Nothing. I was just kidding. It seemed a fun thing to do at the moment."

When they got back to New York, Diane said to Mario, "I have some other friends I want you to meet. They've invited us to dinner. I've told them all about you. They're my favorite people— sort of my ideal. I like the way they live, the kind of relationship they have. They're not ordinary, say, like my parents, but at the same time they're not disturbingly unusual. No one could possibly object to them."

"Sounds like they're neither here nor there."

"Why are you criticizing them when you haven't yet met them?" she asked a little peeved.

"I'm not criticizing them," he said, "only what you say about them."

"They're really very exciting people," she said. "He started out to be a writer. He was very interested when I told him you write. He's in advertising now," she said, "but in his heart he's still a writer."

"What does that mean, in his heart? One is either writing or not."

"Don't get touchy," she said. "What I mean is he couldn't make a living at it, so he had to do something else, but he always wanted to write fiction. There's something to be said for comfort, you know."

"Well, you better say it and get it over with."

"Let's not fight," she said. "I know you're going to like them. They're older people, you know, but they don't seem like it. They keep right up with everything."

On the way to the Kempners, an oppressive silence enveloped them as they waited for the cross-town bus.

"What's the matter?"

"Nothing," he said.

"If I did something, tell me," she insisted.

"It has nothing to do with you," he said.

"What then?"

"I don't know," he said. "Just ignore it. It'll pass."

When they got to the Kempners, Mario put on his charming face. Comfortable people, the Kempners; they looked comfortable, and they acted comfortable. Their apartment was meticulously furnished to produce the effect of good taste indifferently arrived at. They would enthusiastically cheer, from their window, at a demonstration in the street; they admired the younger generation's zeal for peace and love, but lamented its scorn for private property. Sitting in their living room after dinner, Mario was a somewhat enthralled by her manners, and yet their smoothness grated at times. They presented their life with the sleekness of a TV commercial. He wondered how much of their poise depended on their material circumstances. Would they carry themselves with such dignity if suddenly plunged into poverty? The question was absurd, but the negative answer made him feel better.

A few evenings later, after Diane had proposed to spend the night at Mario's, she called: "Some people dropped in unexpectedly. They're old friends from school, and I want to spend a little time with them. I'll be late."

"Okay," he said.

"Are you sure? I mean you're not upset or anything?"

"No, it's all right," he answered.

"You don't sound happy," she said.

"Really, it's all right. I have some work to do anyway."

A few hours later, she called again. "I don't seem to be able to get away," she said. "Why don't you come over here?"

"It's late," he said. "I'd rather stay home."

"Are you sure?"

"Yeah, have a good time."

"I'll see you tomorrow," she said.

"Okay."

He got into bed and read for a while. About to turn off the light, he heard a knock. He went to the door. Night bag in hand, Diane stood there smiling.

"Surprised?"

"Yeah," he said. "And your friends?"

"I just said I had to leave. They kept partying without me."

She began to undress immediately, "I'd rather be with you," she continued.

"I'm glad," he politely said.

"Remember I did this for you," she casually remarked, as she hung her clothes in the closet.

The words were briars to him. "You're scheming," he said.

She turned, her face distorted, every unattractive feature of her countenance emphasized. "Scheming to do what?" she petulantly asked.

"To bind me," he said. "You want me to marry you, don't you?"

"That's preposterous!" She was about to burst into tears. "You've implied that before, and I haven't said anything, because I've been well brought up not to contradict."

"You mean not to contradict men."

"Yes," she said mockingly. "Their egos are too fragile. What makes you think I would want to marry you?"

"I don't know," he said. "Why do you?"

"You want to see other women, don't you? That's what this is about, isn't it?"

"Well, I've thought about it," he said.

"I'm not beautiful," she said. "I know it. I would think that you would want a beautiful woman. Being an artist, you're concerned with beauty."

"Don't be ridiculous," he said. "That has nothing to do with it; but of course, Rachel Fitzgerald is back."

"And you're seeing her now?" she asked in disbelief.

"Yes, of course," he responded using only a partial truth. Rachel had been gone for the summer, but she was back now for the fall term.

"It's her name you're interested in, isn't it? She's related to F. Scott, isn't she?"

"She's not," he said.

"She's not related to the writer?"

"Well, her father is a writer, but not at all related to F. Scott."

"What's he written?"

"I don't know. He uses a pen name."

"He doesn't want to be confused with the real one."

"Listen, that has nothing to do with us," he said.

Diane refrained from casting her fury at him. "Poor Rachel Fitzgerald," she said, "the next victim no doubt. Who will follow Rachel?" She imagined a stream of women taking solace in each other's tears.

# Separate Lives

*O*N FIRST MEETING *THOMAS*, Sandy thought she had found the right man. He was ambitious and wanted to produce quality films, an endeavor that was relevant, artistic, and competitive. In addition, he was good looking. If she had to identify a weakness in herself, the need for a man would immediately emerge. She feared to be without one to call her own. She needed that bond before the eyes of the world, the attachment to a superior man. She married Thomas.

She chose to ignore the quirks in his character that disturbed her, and instead she focused on his obvious strengths. On the first night they spent together, his excessive perspiration discomfited her. She suppressed the impulse to flee, but then, she reasoned, the world is full of anomalies. Perhaps it wasn't a constant condition but merely one due to the stress of the moment, a fear of being judged insufficiently grand. For a while, she relegated the reaction of his sweat glands to the realm of the insignificant, but she opened her eyes one morning to realize that the man lying next to her was the wrong one.

She had fooled herself into thinking that he was essentially different from her father. That was a common enough mistake; often an applicant considered fit at the interview turns out to be wrong for the job. Every day she wondered whether she had really said, "Till death do us part." Why had she failed to see who he really was before she made the commitment, before she said those words? Did she have to stick to them? She had meant them on that day, but now she wanted to delete them from her memory.

For a while, she attempted to minimize the extent of her discomfort. Still, she could not deny her dissatisfaction, her unhappiness, or her knowledge that Thomas was the wrong man. She tried to restore the image that had first attracted her. In that endeavor, her strength of will often produced an adequate result, and she enjoyed it until Thomas inadvertently triggered a collapse of the fiction she had created. She then attempted to convince herself that she was overreacting, but inevitably her inner voice conveyed a different message.

She tried harder. There had to be something in Thomas that would save the day and keep her from making another mistake. She refused to believe that from the beginning she had been deceived. There had to be something in him that validated her original assessment. She couldn't have made so gross an error without some justification. Some of what she had originally concluded had to be correct. His ambitious side had to be admired. In comparison to everyone else, Thomas was a catch, indeed a gem. She told herself that all she needed to do was to get rid of her discomforting doubts.

He would go along way in the world, and she would be there along with him, something to look forward to. That possibility eased her for a time, but she soon saw the fallacy of attaching her personal happiness to his business success. Besides, he had yet to achieve his goal, and she began to doubt that he would. His ambitious side had impressed her, but it had yet to be productive. Yes, he had dreams. He was an entrepreneur, but schemes often lead to nothing and fall apart when facing the realities of the world.

Her faith in him began to shake. She longed for something more ethereal. She had originally thought his goal would be more along an artistic vein. He would be the producer, or maybe even the director, of films fit for the art cinemas. She imagined going to the Thalia or the Bleecker to see the products of his efforts. He had bought the rights to a bestselling novel, but he had yet to get anywhere with it. He would have to raise millions to produce the film, and she began to doubt his ability to do that.

Still, what had that to do with her problem? "For better or for worse," she had said. Certainly, she could imagine worse situations. She could not deny that he loved her. She was sure of that, but she wanted more. Was it ever going to get better with him? She wanted to remove that question, not wait forever for an answer.

She recognized her unhappiness, but she had trouble deciding on an alternative. An inner voice guided her, and she followed with only slight reservation. She was certain of one thing; she did not want to be alone, and she would rather suffer the discomfort of dealing with Thomas than the possible loneliness without him. To be the only one in bed at night, with no one to greet in the morning or welcome home in the evening, aroused fear in her. Then Antonio came along.

§

She met him at a Tuesday night poetry reading at St. Marks, not a usual haunt for her. An acquaintance of a colleague was reading, and as a gesture, she agreed to attend the reading.

Quite unexpectedly something about a young man two rows ahead caught her eye. Observing him became more interesting than listening to the droning emanating from the podium. Words that seemed to have no connection, like some mystical revelation, enraptured the audience, all except this fellow who she had never seen before and in all probability would never see again. At the moment, the smirk on his face fascinated her. It suggested that he took for nonsense what everyone else seemed to revere.

He turned his head and caught her stare. She first interpreted the stretch of his lips as a smile. She saw his right eye momentarily close. Then, he returned his attention to the podium. She wondered whether he had really winked at her. It had been so quick, so brief a moment, followed-up by nothing. She might have imagined the whole sequence or misinterpreted a natural act. Perhaps a speck of dust had stung his eye, and blinking was a natural response. The spreading of his lips may not have been a smile but a grin resulting from the discomfort in his eye. How was she to know?

She would be taking a chance approaching him and asking if his eye was all right. He might take her for a lonely woman trying to pick him up with a lame line, ascribing a bizarre meaning to a natural reaction to the performer at the lectern. Of course, she might just put herself in his line of vision and test whether indeed he had noticed her and had attempted to draw her attention. However, at intermission some other force took over, and she was unable to merely put herself in his line of sight. She advanced to where he stood speaking to someone else and interrupted. The other woman retreated, and Sandy, discounting the rest of the audience, had him all to herself.

"I don't think this reading is going to get any better," he said.

"I think you're right. Did you come to hear a friend read?"

"I came to get a feel for the place. I'm to read here myself next week."

"Ah, a poet," she said.

"No, just a person," he quipped.

"That's even better."

§

The following week, she attended his reading and afterward offered to take him out for a drink.

"Well, a bunch of us already have plans to go out, but you're welcome to join the party."

"I was thinking of a more private happening," she said.

"That too can be arranged. How about tomorrow night?"

"I've already promised to cook for my husband tomorrow," she said.

"Ah, so there's a husband."

"Well, yes, but I have a life of my own."

"Well then, you pick the day."

"Thursday is fine with me."

So, on Thursday night, they met at Monte's on MacDougal Street. On the wall, a seaside scene of some Italian place, possibly Sicily, overwhelmed the décor. Neither one of them knew for sure, and they didn't bother to ask. They had a more interesting subject to discuss.

"And so, what does your husband think about our having dinner without him?"

"I really don't know. I didn't tell him where I was going, and he didn't ask."

"Ah, that's simple enough."

"And what did you tell your partner?"

"Did I say I have one?"

"No, but it's difficult to imagine you without one."

"She's out of town right now," he said.

"That's convenient enough."

"So it is."

After dinner, he offered to walk her home.

"It's still early. Let's walk over to the river," she suggested.

The West Side Highway was still an elevation over West Street, and between Houston and Canal there was only one pier open to the public. When they got there, the sun was setting, and they gazed westward over the water. She stood very close to him, and when they faced each other their noses almost touched. She waited for him to make the move, but he refrained.

"You do live close by, don't you?" she said.

"Just a few blocks."

"Well, are you going to show me your place?"

"Sure," he said.

When they got there, she looked around and was pleased enough, but she wasn't scouting real estate, and she got right to the point.

"At the river, why did you hesitate?"

"You're married," he said.

"I thought that was all right with you."

"I suppose it is."

"Well, then?"

The kiss became inevitable.

"Thomas will be away this Saturday. You and I can spend the day together."

"All right," he said.

"I'll call you in the morning. We can then make definite plans for the day."

He agreed.

§

Saturday morning, Thomas left very early. She stayed in bed and pretended to sleep after he got up. He performed his ablutions and had breakfast. Before he took off, he went by the bed to kiss her. She uttered a slight moan, pretending to still be asleep and his touch had penetrated to some inner realm that automatically responded. She listened to hear the apartment door close after his exit. She waited, allowing time for him to turn the key and then direct his steps to the stairs. She sprang to her feet and over to the telephone to dial Antonio's number.

The phone kept ringing. Wasn't he going to pick-up? Wasn't he home? Where could he have gone so early in the morning? When she finally heard a groggy voice at the other end, she asked, "Well, what's on for today?" She waited for an answer that seemed reluctant to emerge, as if the person at the other end was trying to figure out whose voice was leaping from the receiver into his ear. She suppressed the disappointment of not receiving the welcome she expected. "Well, what is it to be?" she asked. She tried to suppress her annoyance, but like when drinking sugarless coffee, the bitter taste lingered.

"Whatever you like," he said.

She couldn't invite him over to her place. After all, it was also Thomas's place. She would have to deal with that fact at some point, but she wasn't there yet. She wasn't anywhere yet. She had only gone out to dinner with Antonio and had kissed him once. That was nothing. She knew people who routinely exchanged partners, but she wasn't there yet. Of course it was less than a twenty-minute walk to Antonio's, so she might not be that far away after all.

"That's not good enough," she heard herself say while knowing that she was using the wrong tone; her mouth in revolt refused to comply with her wishes.

"Come over," he said.

When she got to his place, she didn't bother to undress before she got into his bed, so he proceeded to slowly disrobe her. When she was fully bare, and he about to undress himself, she said, "Wait a minute. I haven't decided whether to go through with this."

"What the hell is going on here? You've gone this far."

"That's true," she said, and laid her head back on the pillow.

They stayed in bed all morning, and in the afternoon they went to see a very sad movie about the labor struggle in nineteenth century Italy. Marcello Mastroianni played a union organizer who goes to a mill town to organize a strike. There, the local courtesan, the daughter of one of the workers, provides a place to sleep. The struggle gets underway, and the mill owners bring in the army to break the strike. At the end, the organizer is arrested, and his replacement hops a freight out of town on his way to the next battle. The workers have to stay, not much better off than they were before. The movie, sad and real, made her wonder whether Antonio resembled a labor organizer.

Later that day, while they were having supper at a Mexican restaurant, the mariachi band came to their table, and Sandy requested a song Antonio had never heard before.

"How do you know that song?" he asked her.

"Oh, I know lots of songs," she said. "I know more songs than anybody."

She made her claim with great conviction, but she had yet to convince him. After dinner he walked her home.

"Come in and say hello to my husband," she said at the door.

"I think I'll skip that," he said.

"Okay," she said with a grin on her face. "Don't forget to call me."

Before she went up the steps to her apartment, she turned to see Antonio cross the street and proceed down St. Marks.

The next time she was at his place, she noticed that over his desk hung a photograph of another woman.

"You shouldn't keep that picture there," she said pointing at the photograph. "It really bothers me."

"She's my friend," he said.

"Still, I don't want to see her there. You're not being considerate of my feelings, keeping a picture of another woman on your wall."

"What difference does it make? You go home to your husband's bed, don't you?"

"That's different," she said.

"How is it different?"

"It's just different," she insisted. "Just take it down while I'm here."

"All right," he said.

Later in bed she asked him, "Do you mind that I sleep with my husband?"

"No," he said.

"I don't love him, you know."

"Did you ever?"

"No," she said, "not really."

"And you married him anyway?"

"I was impressed by his intelligence."

"And now you're not impressed?"

"I'm still impressed, but there are other things. He sweats in bed. In the morning, he's a puddle of sweat from head to toe. It's disgusting. He didn't like my panties with purple stripes, the ones you said are so exciting. He just thought they were loud. He's no fun that way."

"Sounds like he just needs to loosen up a bit, that's all, but it's none of my business. That's between the two of you," he said.

"That's right. It is, but I want you to understand. He doesn't appreciate me the way you do. He doesn't appreciate my body. He's more into some abstraction of me, and that doesn't feel good."

Yes, that was it. That was the point. She wanted a man that saw her completely. She didn't want to be just a projection of someone's imagination. Thomas was refusing to see her for whom she really was, refusing to see her as an individual entity that existed in a physical world.

"See how my breasts stay upright. I always wear a bra, so they won't sag when I get older," she said to Antonio. "Women with small breasts can burn their bras, but I can't afford to do that. Even though they wouldn't sag now, they would later, and I don't want that to happen."

"That's some forethought," he said.

"You're making fun of me?"

"No, of course not," he assured her.

She convinced herself that he wasn't mocking her.

He wasn't like Thomas. Antonio appreciated her for her sexuality and her knowledge of the world, qualities that Thomas constantly ignored. The problem shifted now that Antonio was the one she wanted. He was the right man for her, the one that she should have waited for. Only, he had yet to express such feelings about her.

"I told my women's group about you," she said to him. "They can't believe how you are in bed. They all want to meet you."

"They want to take turns?"

"I'm sure they do, but I'm sticking close to you. They just want to take a peek at you, so how about it?"

"How about what?"

"Come and pick me up from there, so they can see you."

"Sure, why not," he said. "You know, the more people who know about us, the more difficult it's going to be keeping it from your husband."

"That's all right," she said. "I told him."

"Told him what?"

"That we're lovers."

"Just like that?"

"Yeah."

"You're leaving him?"

"No, not yet."

"Why did you tell him then?"

"I don't know. I just felt like it."

"And what did he do?"

"He cried."

"Jesus! I don't believe this. He cried? That's it? And he continues to live with you?"

"He thinks you seduced me and corrupted me. You have a dark power over me. He doesn't think any of it is my fault."

"That's incredible, and what now?"

"Nothing, we'll go on as we are, and when you decide what your intentions are towards me, I'll decide whether to leave Thomas or not."

"What are you talking about?"

"You have to make a commitment to me before I leave Thomas."

"First you disentangle yourself. Then we'll see where we go from there."

"I can't do that," she said, "I have to be connected to somebody. It's too scary for me to be all alone."

He stared at her in disbelief.

§

The evening crowd was sparse. The summer was already coming to an end as October brought in the cooler weather. A melody from the musicians near the fountain enveloped her. A young man accosted her, withdrawing his hand from his pocket to let her glimpse a small package. Sandy shook her head and continued walking. She noticed a boy laughing loudly in the middle of a group, as he tried to maintain his position as the center of attention.

On getting back to New York, Antonio had agreed to meet her in Washington Square. He had gone across the country to San Francisco in pursuit of the woman whose photograph hung on the wall over his desk. Sandy was eager to see him again, though from the tone of his voice on the phone she had sensed a different Antonio. Gazing across the square, she recognized his gait before distinguishing his features.

Almost as soon as they greeted, she sensed that this was

to be their last encounter. She had never before known him to be intransigent, and she interpreted his new mood as his no longer loving her. She saw his fear of falling into the same predicament as Thomas, and she stopped trying to make him understand that she would never do that to him.

"You're still in love with her," she said, referring to the woman in the photograph in search of whom he had gone to San Francisco.

"She's gone," he retorted.

"She'll never be gone."

"Maybe not, but that's irrelevant."

Sandy saw that he wanted to make that the truth, but she doubted that he would ever succeed.

"Anyway, we can't go on like this," he finally said.

"You're right," she said.

They walked together arm in arm to the edge of the park, then parted to separate lives.

# An Occupied Bench

"*WHAT TOOK YOU* so long?" Ellen asked when Henry finally brought himself to call.

"I didn't want to seem too hasty," he quipped.

"What did you have in mind?"

"Let's have lunch," he said.

"You were right to play it cool," she said. "I often turn guys down who invite me to lunch too eagerly."

"I don't always sound like a jerk," he said.

"I hope not," she replied, "or lunch is going to be very tedious."

On picking her up at her office, he scrutinized her surroundings as he waited for her to conclude a business call. Her business suit struggled to conceal that she was the same woman he had met two weeks before. At the moment, she presented a different image than the one he remembered. He had previously perceived her as a softer person, but now he was confronted with an impeccable style executed with precision.

In the restaurant, where they declined the enclosed veranda and opted to sit in the back, a smile hovered at the corners of her mouth.

"So you were married once," she said.

"That amuses you?" he asked.

"Everything about you amuses me."

"It wasn't very amusing to me, but at least it's over."

"Is it ever over?" she asked. "Some have a point when they say marriage is forever. Isn't it imprinted on your soul—the fact that you were married to a particular person? And there is nothing that can erase an imprint on the soul. Not even the Pope can do it."

"That's a morbid thought."

"No, not at all," she responded. "It's really quite beautiful."

"She and I were never meant for each other. The whole thing was a mistake from beginning to end. Does that mean I have a mistake imprinted on my soul forever?"

"Well, yes," she said laughing. Seeing, however, that he wasn't amused, she tried to contain her mirth. "Really, tell me what your wife is like," she said as they waited for the waiter.

"My ex-wife, you mean."

"Yes her."

"Why are you so interested in the past? The future is much more interesting."

"It's a game I play," she said. "I imagined what kind of a woman you were married to, and I want to see how close I came. I want to see if my impression of you is correct."

"If I tell you about my wife, it will only lead you astray."

"Was she so bad?"

"She may not have been so bad, but she and I were awful together."

It was difficult to describe the awfulness without being unfair. He wanted so much to be fair, but he found it difficult to discard the anger at what seemed to him a betrayal. Yet, he knew that the matter was not that simple. She had only been herself—a self that had been there for him to see all along.

His failure had not resulted completely from not knowing her, but also in large part from not knowing himself. "She was a hypochondriac," he said.

"Ah, always complaining."

"Not so much complaining as demanding special consideration—a way of avoiding responsibility—because she was sick."

"Well, was she sick or not?"

"Not physically," he said.

"You don't sound sure."

"Who can be sure of anything?" he said.

"Who indeed?"

He was not finding this conversation easy. It no longer seemed one to one. There was more than one woman here confronting him, perhaps a whole array of women who refused to let him get away with his uncertainty.

"Enough about me," he said. "Let's hear about you. How does married life suit you?"

"How do I look?"

"Terrific," he said.

"Well, there you are."

"That's not the answer I was looking for," he said.

"What then?"

"I was hoping that you were terribly unhappy and married to an ogre from whom I could save you and be your hero."

"And at the end I would throw myself under a train."

"You can't know the end before getting through the beginning."

"Why not?" she asked. "I already know what I want for dessert."

He had the sensation of riding a roller coaster. He tried

to reassure himself that he was in no danger, but the feeling of panic resisted rational control. Looking into her pale blue eyes, her round face framed by yellow hair pulled tightly back into a bun, he saw nothing that would normally cause alarm. Her earrings, simple gold knots, and the pearls around her neck bespoke only of restrained elegance. He was not sure whether to press on with questions about her marriage. Did he really want to hear the details of her blissful domesticity? He sipped from his wine glass as if to restrain the passing of time, but it was no use. He was compelled to discard caution. Like a man standing at the edge of a precipice, if he stepped forward it would be into an abyss that at that moment seemed interminable but exhilarating.

"What is he like, your husband?"

She did not respond immediately, and he wondered whether she was trying to spare him the pain of hitting the bottom of the canyon.

"He's all right," she said.

"Yes, he must be."

"You're quite all right too," she said with an impish smile.

The waiter sauntered to their table. "The specials for today..." he began.

Ellen seemed to listen attentively, but Henry was still trying to decide whether to take her words at face value. The suspicion grew that she was misinforming him about the condition of her marriage. He glanced up at the young man rattling the list of dishes.

"If you need a few more minutes, I can come back," the waiter said on seeing the befuddlement on Henry's face.

"That would be good," Ellen said, bestowing upon the

boy a studied but charming smile. After he had moved away, she said ever so gently, "The menu is not that complicated."

"No, it's not," Henry said, "but it sometimes seems like it is." With that he sensed that he had taken a step in the right direction, as if having been lost in a marsh he felt at long last firm ground under his feet. It was but a first step, and there was no assurance that with the next he would not again be knee deep in mire. But the one sure step buoyed his spirit, and he was willing to go on. He would not have been able to say, had he been asked, what sign she had given him to so dramatically alter his mood. He wondered whether he was reading more into her expressions than was reasonable; whether in his eagerness to find his way, he was inventing signs to confirm his progress.

"Let me tell you what's good here," she said, taking the menu and evaluating each item in the most amusing restaurant review he had ever heard.

She made him laugh, and he caught a glimpse of the woman he had previously imagined. For an instant, she let down her mask for him see that there was something else behind the appearance, a conspirator letting a partner know that behind the disguise there was someone else. It was this sense of conspiracy that allowed him to see his way clear, or rather, to see his way dimly, for in no sense was he yet in the clear. What he did see was that she was hiding and that she wanted him to know that. He was left on his own, however, to figure out what she wanted him to do about it, if anything. On that point, he saw no urgency but was content to enjoy for a moment the relief of not having to consider her dangerous, or at any rate, immediately menacing.

He took a few minutes to navigate the menu, and with

her help came to a simple decision as to what to have for lunch. He managed this expeditiously enough, so that on the waiter's return he was able to order with the dispatch and authority worthy of a man of the world, a task which he was normally able to perform quite well on his own.

He wanted to see whether she would open the door further—a door that she had left ajar just enough to give him a tantalizing glimpse. If she wanted him to come in, she would have to open the door further, for he was not the sort of person to force his way. He was not even, like an aggressive salesman, willing to put his foot in jeopardy.

"You know," he said, "you seem quite a different person today than you were when we first met."

"What do you mean?" she asked.

"I mean," he said, "that I don't know quite what to make of you."

"You're making me out to be more mysterious than I really am," she said.

"I don't mean to say you're mysterious, only that you're perplexing."

"I'm not simple you mean."

"I mean that, yes."

"I think you can handle a little complexity," she assured him.

"Well, you're taking that on faith."

"Yes, I am doing that," she said, shifting a burden onto him and waiting to see whether he would accept it. She watched with heightened interest as he squirmed somewhat, trying to find a proper equilibrium for the load. He showed no sign of immediately dropping it, nor did he make any verbal complaint.

He was content to let this perplexity fade into the background, pushed there and buried by an avalanche of effervescent small talk, at which she was, expectably, a master. She had put him in, and he had accepted a role with which he was familiar and comfortable. As the recipient of her faith, he had no problem, like the straw man, in whiling away the hours. When the waiter asked if they wished to see the dessert menu, Henry was surprised, on looking around, that his surroundings were indeed the same as when he had walked in. He covered up his amusement, so he would not have to explain, complimentary as his lapse from the time and place might have been to her.

It was she who, on their way back, came around again to the more serious part of their conversation. "I hope," she said, "that I haven't asked too much of you."

"I think I can bear too much better than not enough," he said.

"It's not a question of what you can bear, but of what you're willing to."

"In either case you need not fear," he replied.

"I am grateful for that," she said. "Do call me again."

He concluded, as he watched the omnivorous elevator swallow her, that gratitude was due.

When he answered the phone two days later, he was pleased to hear her voice. Her initiative relieved him of responsibility for the next step.

"I'll pick you up," he offered.

"No, I'll meet you there," she said.

Before he agreed, a momentary silence pervaded as he realized the awkwardness of the situation. He did not dwell on it, but the pause became one more sign that he was not in complete control. He was glad the she gave no sign of being aware of his hesitancy. When he arrived, she was already at the door of the concert hall sparing him the anxiety of having to wait for her.

At the end of the concert, he had to face the music. "You know this is all very strange," he said.

"What is?"

"Our relationship," he answered.

"What relationship is that?"

"You tell me."

"This is not something to discuss in public," she said. "Why don't you take me home with you, so that we can resolve the matter?"

§

"Here we are at last," she said when they got to his place, and she looked around to see whether it was all she had imagined.

"Well, is it what you expected?" he asked. He was curious to hear what her fantasy had been. He hoped it would give him a clue as to what her expectations might be.

"To tell you the truth," she said, "I'm rather surprised. I'm usually not so wrong."

"How wrong are you?" he asked, sensing that he might for the first time have the advantage in an exchange with her.

"It might be that I'm all wrong," she said sitting down on the leather couch. She was not, however, to be denied for very long, and her sense of mischief was always to be counted on to rescue her from potentially disconcerting situations. "Or I might be completely right," she said triumphantly, as if she had narrowly escaped from an unforeseen disaster. "Yes, I'm right. This is not you."

He knew that he had her now, because looking around he saw only himself. He had in fact, after his divorce made it a point to indulge in the furnishing of his home. There was nothing in it that was even slightly reminiscent of anything his former wife would have favored.

"It's not you," she said again.

He did not press her further to reveal what she had expected, knowing that she would tell him as soon as she recovered the image that she had unconsciously assumed.

"You think too much," she said. "Isn't that dangerous?"

"Only if I had a lean and hungry look."

"You do," she said. "That's what this place is telling me."

"Ah, the decor," he exclaimed as if he understood what she meant.

She waited for him to elaborate, but he kept silent. He had no idea what she was talking about.

"I can help you," she said.

"I suppose you can," he retorted, "You've helped me a great deal already."

"No, I haven't," she said.

"Then I must be in much more trouble than I thought."

He sat down next to her, and she turned to face him. She wanted to answer him, but she saw that there was no need. For the first time since they had met, he touched her in more than a handshake. He half expected her to recoil from him, but she refused to retreat.

The complications of the situation could not be put off even on their first night together, and though she did not hesitate to get into his bed, neither did she apologize when she announced that she could not stay the night. He had understood that she had another commitment, but it was uncomfortable to find it so pressing. He did not want to seem unsophisticated, and he assumed that sophistication meant taking the inconvenience in stride. And if that were all that he felt, an inconvenience, he would not have been far wrong. But he was no longer sure of what he felt, if he had ever been, now that he was watching her get dressed again, and each article of clothing that she put on represented a withdrawal from him.

He could not refrain, however, from asking, "What will you say to your husband about where you've been?"

"He won't ask," she said, "but I'll tell him the truth. I was at a concert. He won't ask who I was there with, and I won't ask about where he was or with whom."

"You have an arrangement then."

"We have an understanding."

He pondered what the difference might be, and concluded that it was not his business to understand their understanding, as long as he was getting what he wanted. It came down to that. He had to decide what he wanted sooner or later, but it didn't have to be at that very instant. So what he was left with at the moment was good enough. He was not, after all, certain that he wanted more, if more was to be had, and the prospect of getting less was just an irksome possibility.

There were questions, nevertheless, that remained half formed at the back of his mind, questions about a world where husband and wife had such understandings, and why it would seem such an oddity to him. He asked himself whether he would have preferred that she were merely cheating. At least then he could assume a reason that would be understandable even to the most common person. The criterion was absurd, he knew, under any circumstances.

She sensed his discomfort though she was not sure of its cause. "I'm not leaving forever," she said.

"No, not forever," he echoed.

She searched for what else to say that might comfort him, then she said without quite knowing why, "Would you like to meet my husband sometime?"

He did not think it seemly to display just how much the idea appealed to him, so he dissembled a little, just as much as he thought he could get away with. "That would be rather awkward, don't you think?"

"Only if you tell him you've been screwing me."

"Ah," he said, thinking that might be exactly what she would like him to do, "I'll let you tell him."

She did not reply to that, as no reply was necessary. "It shouldn't be difficult to arrange," she said. "It can be as if by accident. We can meet in a public place. I think it would be great fun."

"Great fun for us, you mean?"

"Yes, for us," she said.

"What about him? He won't know what's going on, will he?"

"No, he won't unless you want him to, in which case you might clue him in."

"I think not," he said.

"That's all right, too."

"Well then he'll be missing out on all the fun, won't he?"

"Not exactly," she said. "He gets to walk away with me."

"I suppose he does."

"That must add up to some fun," she said, "though not as much as ours."

"Really?"

"Not by a long shot," she said, "but does it matter?"

"It matters to him."

"I mean does it make any difference to you whether he has fun with me?"

"No, not in the least."

"It's all set then. I'll call and tell you where to meet us. Just act casually as if you were there coincidentally."

This was the kind of stunt, he was sure, that was likely to blow up in one's face, but he did not say anything to her. It was a lark. He could plainly see that it was something she would relish. It was an adventure they would have together, and he did not want to disappoint her. But it was not just that, the going along for her sake. He was genuinely curious to meet her husband, and though he was not quite comfortable in doing it under false pretenses, he did not nix the plan.

"I'll call you," she said again, as she boarded the taxi he had called to take her home.

He didn't go back to his place after the taxi pulled away but walked down Fifth Avenue to Washington Square, where late in the evening there was an abundance of life, the sort that had ragged edges and unusual textures.

He sat down on a park bench to contemplate the scene around him. In the night, the images of his personal purgatory abounded. He sat there observing what he thought were shattered lives; people who existed on the fringes of society, except for the students who attended the university that boarded the square. They hung out in the park for the thrill of doing something their parents would object to. He saw a young woman whom he imagined as having grown up in a suburban ranch house and who now, away from the prying eyes of her parents, associated with people with whom her father would be outraged to see her, and for whom her fiancé, present or future, would have contempt. He wondered about the extent of the relationships played out in the park. Would this girl, at the end of her routine, go home with one of these desperate characters? He imagined it must be so, though his scruples recoiled at the thought. He contemplated the possibility that it was only the encounter in the park that she was after, that at the end she would go back to the ordinary, the safety of her dormitory. He hoped that he was being fair to the desperate characters. They were, after all, people too, who had their stories, their longings and desires and their struggle for survival just as much as anybody else. Who was to blame if in the scheme of fate they had landed on the wrong side of the tapestry?

A homeless man approached and sat beside him on the bench. Henry resisted the impulse to get up and walk away.

"You're sitting on my bench," the vagabond said, revealing gums with missing teeth.

"Oh?"

"I'm not asking you to move, you understand, I'm just letting you know that it's my bench you're sitting on."

"Well, is there any bench in this park that isn't yours?" Henry asked.

"No, there ain't," the homeless man said, cackling from the bottom of his belly. Henry, too, was forced to smile. It was a friendly laugh that diffused the tension of two strangers meeting after dark in a city park.

"Woman trouble, huh?"

"What makes you say that?"

"I know woman trouble when I see it. I had woman trouble all my life. Wouldn't be here right now but for woman trouble. Ain't no way to get around it though; just got'a live through it, and come out on the other side. I ought'a know. Whatever kind of woman trouble there is, I've been through it."

"I'm sure you have," Henry said.

"No you ain't," the homeless man said, "just like you don't believe this is my bench, but it is."

Henry pulled out some change from his pocket, and passed it on. "For the use of your bench," he said.

The vagabond chuckled, then hobbled away to make his claim to the next occupied bench.

# Literary Affairs

*A*T THE OFFICE, Joan spreads the most outrageous gossip. The other day she told me that Audrey Thurman, for the past two years, has been having an affair with Mark Shaw. A married woman having an affair is common enough, but Audrey had not seemed the type. She's not a great beauty, but I find her very enticing, and I've fantasized about her.

"She seems so nun-like," Joan said.

"Not exactly," I rejoined, although I recognized the quality that Joan was alluding to. "She just seems so level headed, like someone who has everything in place and abides by the rules."

"And he's such a slime ball," Joan said. "In fact, he's worse than slime."

Coming from Joan, that was a rather ironic statement. In her own amorous relationships, she prefers uneducated working class men who don't quite fit into the rest of her life. After all, she is an intellectual working at a publishing house. So, most of her friends are rather staid, but not her sexual partners.

She used to date a very parsimonious guy. He never had any money when they went out, and she would end up picking up the tab. He would stay with her and consume her groceries, never contributing to the household expenses. A few times, he delved into her purse for cash. Eventually, she had to get rid of him. The next guy was no better; he was an embarrassment. Her agent gave a big party where she was to work the room and possibly get some TV producers interested in her book. He asked her not to bring her boyfriend, who clearly did not fit into that crowd. "He is kind of stupid," she admitted to me, "but what the hell."

She met the current lover on the subway. She ran into him several times on her way to work, and she initiated the relationship. That is, she surprised him by asking him out. He said he had noticed her but never made a move because he thought she wouldn't be interested in a guy like him.

"He's Puerto Rican, and he works as a bouncer in a nightclub," she told me.

"Just your kind of guy," I said.

"Isn't he? He calls me all the time, and he tells me how much he likes me. I like that," she said. "And guess how many eggs he eats for breakfast."

"Four," I said, thinking that was an outrageous number of eggs for anyone to eat at one time.

"I mean how many did he used to eat before I got him to cut down?" she said.

"I don't know," I said. "How many?"

"A whole dozen," she said. "I told him that was too many eggs to eat at one meal, and he said he would eat seven. I said he had to go down to four. He did, but he still has a whole slab of bacon with the eggs."

"Incredible," I said. "How big is this guy?"

"He weighs three hundred and ten pounds. He looks about five ten, but he's really six three. He's just so wide that he looks shorter than he actually is. I told him he has to eat three helpings of fruit and vegetables a day. Once, he called to tell me he ate three bananas all at one time. Can you believe that? He wants to get a job as a bouncer in a nightclub up in East Harlem, so I told him that then he doesn't have to worry about his cholesterol, because he'll probably die of gunshot wounds."

"Why did you say that? Puerto Ricans are very calm people. There's never any trouble up there," I said.

"Yeah, right."

"Sure, very calm people."

"You're the only calm Puerto Rican I know."

§

The next time I spoke to her, she was very upset. "I'm so depressed," she said. "I'm just upset at the whole world."

"Why is that?"

"I had to go to the police station last night, and that's such a depressing place."

I waited for her to tell me why she had gone to the police.

"It happened again," she said. "My guy stole from me. I couldn't believe it; my fat Puerto Rican bouncer stole money from me."

"So you had him arrested. That's good."

"No, no, I didn't want him arrested. I told the police not to arrest him, and they were upset at me. 'We have enough on him to arrest him,' they said. I don't want him arrested. He has a dying mother. 'So what are you doing here?' they asked me. I just want it on record in case anything else happens, in case he hurts me, or something. 'What makes you think he might hurt you? Did he threaten you?' Well, a few weeks ago he said, 'I'm a trained killer,' because he was a marine. 'I could snap someone's neck with no trouble at all. I don't do it, because I'm a nice guy, but I could do it if I want to.' That's what he said, so I just want it on record.

'Well, we're not a record keeping company. We should just arrest him.' But I said no. His sister is getting the money for me."

"You mean she's paying you what he took?"

"She's making him give her the money, and she's returning it to me in installments. It turns out that he's a coke addict. That's why he took the money. I sure know how to pick them. My ghetto boys always turn out bad. But what can I do? I'm attracted to them."

§

Doris recently gave birth, and she has not yet lost all the weight she gained during pregnancy, so she is a little on the heavy side. Normally she is trim. She dresses well, and she's good looking except that she consistently colors her hair blond; otherwise she is tasteful and stylish. She suffers from depression, but the condition is not obvious.

She's a lot younger than I am. I suspect she looks at me as a father figure. We each work in a different group, and we had no occasion to speak to each other in the normal course of our workday. I was at Inwood for two years before we spoke to each other. I said hello a couple of times, then one day I just said, as we passed in the corridor, "We have to have lunch one day."

"Yes," she said enthusiastically. "We have to."

I was surprised by her eager response, as if she had been waiting for me to make the suggestion. So right after Joan told me about Audrey's affair with Mark Shaw, I had lunch with Doris.

"Have you heard about Audrey and Mark?" she asked.

"Yes," I said, "I was shocked."

"I was surprised also," she said. "I can't think of a more unlikely couple."

"I haven't heard very good things about him," I said.

"I can't say anything bad," Doris said. "We worked on the same project once, and he seemed like a nice guy. That's when he was still a consultant. The only negative thing that I can say is that he is somewhat insecure. When he heard that I was assigned to check his work, he got furious. But he did calm down after I explained to him what I was doing. He was all right with it after that, and we got along fine."

"Do you know Audrey's husband?" I asked. "They seemed an ill match."

"He's a very loud and uncouth sort of person, very much the opposite of Mark."

"And Audrey always struck me as being elegant, so when I met her husband I was surprised, but I said to myself, 'Well there is no rhyme or reason about these things.'"

"There isn't," she said, "I know from experience."

"Are they getting a divorce?"

"She's got one already," Doris said. "Mark was the cause."

"The lover is never the cause," I said.

She disagreed. "A woman can be very attracted to a man who is the opposite of what she's used to. I'm sure Mark is the sort of guy who sends her flowers and quotes poetry to her, all the things her husband is incapable of doing."

I think all that stuff is superficial and doesn't really determine anything, but I didn't say so to Doris.

§

As Judith came out of a meeting in the conference room, Joan ran up to her and told her that the cover for the paperback edition of her novel had arrived, and she wanted to show it to her. They were all smiles, and they went to Joan's office to examine the artwork.

What's wrong with this picture? Nothing you say, just two friends talking about success.

Joan tells me the most awful things about Judith: that she's absolutely cheap, that she has no heart, and that her position was bought for her by her husband, who is cronies with the upper management. So why all the smiles and chumminess?

Joan always attends the Christmas party. Groups of us walk from the office to wherever the party is taking place, usually a nearby bar. Joan had asked me to wait for her so we might walk together, but then she changed her mind. She seemed a little uncomfortable and made some excuse about why I should go on without her. It was no big deal to me, but it piqued my curiosity. It soon became clear that she wanted to make an entrance at the party in the company of certain people. She wanted to be seen as part of a particular group, the young executive women of the division, among whom Judith was prominent.

At first I was a little ticked off that she would throw me over just to make an entrance with that group, but I realized that she is just trying to survive in a competitive world. She's too insecure about her ability to do her job, though she would be able to do it well enough if she acquired some confidence. Sometimes I think she is not aware of what she is doing, but at some level she is, because she feels guilty. She tries to compensate by being outspoken and critical of those very people she wants to be seen with. She tells me the most outrageous things she says to them, though I have never heard her doing it. If we put her friendship with Judith in that context, everything makes sense.

Another useful technique she exploits is friendship with the secretaries, who have a great deal of information about what goes on behind closed doors. Much of the gossip that Joan passes on comes from them. I don't mean to say that Joan cynically exploits these people, not even Judith. In some ways she gives as much as she takes. It's really a very skillful symbiosis.

§

Oblivious of the world around her, June Hardy talks to herself. She walks down the corridor deep in conversation, but there is no one near her. We are all capable of withdrawing into our imaginations, but most of us know enough to do it more covertly. In her late fifties, June is single and lives alone. She and Henry Anson used to be very close friends. They always had lunch together, and we would all joke about how they were probably having an affair. Perhaps they were, but just because people often have lunch together doesn't mean they're romantically involved, though maybe they want to be.

Possibly, all that was going on between June and Henry was a lunchtime friendship, but after years of being friends, they suddenly stopped. Now they don't even speak to each other.

"Have you noticed that Henry and June are no longer an item?" I asked Joan.

"Who hasn't," she said, "and do you know why?"

"I have no idea."

"It was Wilson's doing. He said to Henry that if he wanted to keep his position, he'd better stop making a fool of himself in front of the whole company, he being a married man and all."

§

The first thing one notices about Jay Wilson is his bulk. He's a fat man, not as fat as some, but fat enough. He walks with a little bounce as if he were a giant balloon intermittently rolling and bouncing along. If he's in a good mood his whole face looks jolly, and his blue eyes sparkle above his puffy cheeks. When he's in a bad mood, everything about him looks leaden. His shoulders droop; his face contracts at the center producing a snout.

Usually he's wonderfully pleased with himself. He tries to illustrate his points with what he thinks are clever stories or witticisms.

"If two people are driving to California, who should decide what route to take?" he asks.

I know it's a trick question, but I humor him by answering honestly. "If two people are going, they decide together," I say.

"Wrong," he says. "The driver decides."

Each answer presupposes a different set of premises, opposing outlooks on life. One assumes cooperation is the most efficient way to accomplish a task. The task is paramount. The other puts the imposition of will as the first order of business. The task of getting to California becomes secondary. In a corporation, showing that you can impose your will on other people seems the best way to get ahead.

Sometimes he latches on to a currently popular phrase, and he repeats it over and over as if he can't get over how clever the phrase is, as if he had coined it himself. I hear him say: "He talks the talk, but does he walk the walk?" Inwardly,

I wince every time he says it in its several variations, for instance, "I've heard him talk the talk, but I haven't seen him walk the walk."

Of course some people think well of him; Doris for instance. Recently, she hadn't been feeling well, and I went by her office to see how she was doing.

"Hello, Mrs. Grabble," I said to her.

"Hello, Mr. Banderas," she said to me turning from her work.

"How are you today?"

"Much better, thank you. I don't know whether I had a virus or whether I had food poisoning."

"Did you eat in the cafeteria?"

"Actually I didn't lunch at all yesterday and had very little breakfast. I'm trying to lose weight. It must've been a virus. You know, Wilson was very nice to me. I was going to go home and he said, 'First I'll get someone to take you to medical. I'm not letting you go home like this.' He was very solicitous. And today he came by to see how I was. I thought that was very nice. I never had much to do with him before."

"He can be very nice," I said. "He can be the opposite too. It depends on what mood he's in."

"Yes, I've heard that about him," she said.

§

It's altogether possible that Jay was involved in the split between June and Henry, but unlikely, so I queried Joan about her conclusion. "How do you know it was Jay who came between Henry and June?" I asked her.

"I have my sources," she answered.

Presumably such a conversation between Henry and Jay

was private, and neither Henry nor Jay would have revealed it to Joan, which leaves only her imagination as the source.

"And have you noticed what it's done to June?" Joan continued. "She aged considerably since the breakup."

"No, I haven't noticed," I said. "She's no spring chicken anyway."

"No, but she was remarkably well preserved until this happened. That relationship was everything to her. She had nothing else in her life. It was very cruel of Jay to do that."

Joan's voice revealed genuine concern for June, though she often professes to hate her with a passion. Neither of them can abide the aberrations of the other. June is intolerably boring, and Joan is overly brash. Joan fears that June's boring outlook might somehow contaminate her, and June fears, not without cause, that Joan's brashness is dangerous. June is a true nerd. Her ability to do and enjoy her work is the only source of status that she can put before the world. She talks about her work incessantly, going on and on about minutiae that is interesting to no one but herself. Joan couldn't care less about such things, but unlike most people who out of politeness allow June some latitude, Joan only shows contempt.

In my office yesterday, June mentioned Henry Anson. I took the opportunity to ask about the change in their relationship.

"You and Henry are not as friendly as you used to be," I said.

"Ah, yes, things do change," she said. "We had a falling out."

"What happened?" I asked.

"Apparently there are things one isn't supposed to talk

about and much less complain about," she said. "Remember when I was upset about the inadequate air conditioning during the summer? There was no air in here. What is one supposed to do? Keep quiet and not breathe? Henry didn't think I should have complained so vociferously. I suppose he wanted to curry favor with Jay."

She told me about having had a lover in her youth. They had stayed together for some years, but finally the relationship proved unworkable. His name was Eric. His father owned a New England shipyard where they built sailing yachts. Eric loved to sail, but he hated to work. Though perhaps, it was not work that he abhorred but responsibility. As long as he could sail, he didn't mind living by the seat of his pants. He didn't mind genteel poverty as long as he had the boat, and the boat ate up a lot of money, but he was happy just to sail.

June grew up in a suburb of Los Angeles. She took comfort for granted. Eric was an experiment, but she fell in love with him. She thought his life style odd, but the novelty of it kept her going for a while. Eventually, she realized that he wasn't going to change, and she would always have to take care of practical matters. She wasn't up for it. Life in New England working class towns was not her idea of a good time. She was smart enough to know that love couldn't survive economic insecurity. After a few years, they split up. Eric went on to marry a wealthy woman. That solved his problem. What he had always needed was someone to look after him financially. June had loved him, but she did not regret the separation. The price of keeping him would have been too great, and she would have hated him eventually.

§

The very first conversation I had with Doris after she

came back from maternity leave was about how happy she was to be a mother, but that she wasn't sure that she wanted to stay with her husband. He was a very good man, she assured me, but he lacked a certain dynamism that she craved.

"Well," I said, "it's hard for one man to be all things."

"I suppose you're right," she said. "I think I've changed a great deal on that subject. When I was married to Steve, my previous husband, I never would have contemplated having an affair. Now, I think it may be the answer. If I had known enough to just have an affair with Erik, I would still be married to Steve and everything would be all right."

Steve was overbearing and controlling. She had deferred to him completely, and in return she expected him to take care of everything and make her feel safe. In short, she had substituted Steve for a father. When things were good with him, she was on a high, but the opposite often happened.

She met Erik. He was a Romantic. He wrote her poetry, and he sent her flowers. He swept her off her feet. She left Steve. She would have left him sooner or later. She was growing up, but she thought she was leaving because of Erik. She wanted unconditional and absolute love from her new man. When he was hesitant, she began to reevaluate his virtues. Steve was forceful. He was an intellectual who did not beat around the bush. He was witty and charming, a man who dominated the conversation, who filled up every room he walked into. She concluded that she had made a mistake, but it was too late to go back. Steve had found someone else. His new girlfriend worked as a cleaning woman, and she hardly spoke English.

"How could he lower himself so?"

"Well, that's what imagination is for," I said. "A good fantasy life goes a long way."

"I can't do that," she said. "I need the real thing."

"I think the other works better. I saw a good movie the other day called *Nina Take a Lover*. I think you'll find it interesting."

I also recommended *Doña Flor and Her Two Husbands*, but I doubted that solution would satisfy her.

§

"Your little Austrian friend is very seductive," Joan said to me referring to Doris. "I'm seductive, but she's a hundred times more seductive than me, in a different way of course. We have different styles, but she is something else."

"She's not kidding," I said. "She's serious."

"That's right. She's looking for a lover."

"She's only been married to this guy a year."

"She hates the guy. She went into the marriage hating him. Everything about him makes her skin crawl. That's a form of hate. She knew it when she married him. He never does anything right in her eyes. The way he wears his tie or the shirt he puts on always bothers her. Now she thinks the other one was the right one. He was arrogant and mistreated her, but that's what she wants. When a man treats her nicely, she takes it as a sign of weakness. She'll never be happy with anyone. She doesn't have the self-awareness to know what she's doing nor the analytical skills to figure it out."

"You're right," I said.

Just at that moment, Judith came by. She was wearing a very smart pantsuit.

"Did you see this?" Joan said, taking out a copy of the paperback edition of her novel about to be released.

"Oh, it looks great," Judith said. "It looks like you."

On the cover of the book was a close-up of a woman's face. The photo resembled Joan, only much younger. The dark glasses on the cover model were exactly the kind Joan wore.

"Of course, I don't know what it has to do with what the book is about."

"It doesn't matter," Joan said. "It just has to look cool."

"Speaking of cool, how do you like my lipstick?"

The shade was a very pale pink.

"I was just about to fix my own," Joan said. "It's the same color." She took out her lipstick and began to apply it, looking in the small mirror she kept on the wall near her desk. The color, however, was darker than Judith's.

"That's not the same color," Judith said. "This is the cool color," she said addressing me. "This I what everyone is wearing. I have to tell you a story," she said turning to Joan. A cue for me to leave, but I didn't. "I went out with a friend last night, and she drank a little too much. She got tipsy."

"Plastered?" I asked.

"Yeah, absolutely. She was feeling depressed because… well that's another story."

I figured she didn't want to talk about her friend in front of me. It was probably someone Joan knew also.

"Anyway, she ordered an ice cream sundae, and it spilled all over her. I mean right on her lap," she made a circular gesture in front of her own lap to indicate the extent of the damage. "Then my husband tried to clean her up. We all helped to clean her up. Then there were all the jokes about cleaning her crotch. We were quite a ruckus in a rather nice restaurant. Afterwards, we all went to my place to smoke cigars."

"Ugh, that's disgusting," Joan said. "I can't stand the smell of cigars."

"I like the smell," Judith said, "and I looked so cool smoking my husband's cigars."

"I have something to tell you," Joan said. "I was just about to throw this guy out."

"No, no, I don't want to interrupt," Judith protested.

"It's all right," Joan said. "I'll tell you on the way to the rest room. I have to fix my makeup."

§

Doris came by my office.

"How are you?" I said. She looked very stylish in a blue and white-striped jacket.

"I'm going to be out next Monday and Tuesday. Alex and I are going to the resort where we went for our honeymoon. We decided it would be a good tradition to go there every year on our anniversary."

"That's very romantic," I said.

"I hope the weather is good. There's nothing to do there when the weather isn't nice."

"Well, you can always stay in your room and...." I was about to say, "recreate your honeymoon," but she interrupted.

"Get real," she said. "I'm going there with my husband."

We both laughed. "What a thing to say," I exclaimed.

"Well, he's not here. I can say it," she retorted smiling as if it were the most natural thing in the world to think of her husband as a dullard.

The next time I went by her desk, she didn't hear me approach, and she was startled.

"What's up?" she asked.

"Just came by to say, hello," I said.

"Hello," she curtly followed.

"How are you?"

"Getting by," she said, "just trying to balance my checkbook."

"Let's make a date," I said.

She reached for her appointment book, but thought better of it. "I'll call you," she said.

"All right," I said and walked away.

Not very long after, she and her husband were in a custody battle over their infant daughter.

"I can't believe how devious he is," she said to me. "I was so gullible to think he would stick to our verbal agreement. Suddenly, he hired a lawyer, and he's taking me to court."

She was finding out about him the hard way.

"How can he treat me this way?" she said. "After I've been so reasonable."

A few days later, on my way out to lunch, I ran into her in the lobby by the elevator. She was wearing a very interesting outfit.

"That's a very sexy outfit," I said.

Unhesitatingly, she unbuttoned the jacket and opened it up to show me the see-through blouse with nothing underneath but her bra.

"I'll stop by," I said, but that day I never got around to it.

# Modern Art

*A*s *THEY SAT* in metallic chairs at an angle to each other in the sculpture garden of the Museum of Modern Art, Raymond Cassario said to his friend Zachary Goodwin "I'm not sure that I know what I'm doing."

"Do you mean that you don't know what the ultimate outcome will be, or that you don't know what you want it to be?" Zachary Goodwin asked opting to keep the conversation serious.

"You see the depth of my problem, don't you? I don't even know the answer to that question."

"This is different from the usual," Zachary said.

The sculpture garden was one of their favorite places to sit and talk, though often they just sat there silently contemplating the serenity of the surroundings. Zachary felt a contradiction between the feeling of the place and the fact that it was dedicated to modernity. The implications of the word "modern" created a problem for him, a discord. The word had a liability, an inescapable affinity to time; a placing of it at the very end of the stream while simultaneously evoking everything that went before.

The garden had an opposite effect on Raymond. It provided him with a feeling of timelessness, or rather, a serenity that he associated with being outside of time. At the moment, he had a sense of not having moved since they had first sat there as boys. He could not deny that many changes, internal and external, had occurred since then. The external ones were too obvious: now they both were groomed more conservatively, and they had both grown rounder; Zachary more so, though in his youth, he had been the athlete. Those changes, however, were insignificant in comparison to the less obvious ones, the ones they had to ascertain in the same manner physicists deal with elementary particles— indirectly.

"Yes, this is different," Raymond concurred with his friend's assessment.

"You are perplexed."

"Is that what you think is different? I've been perplexed before."

"You've been mistaken before," Zachary said, "but you've kept perplexity well hidden."

"Showing it is the difference, you say?"

"That too," Zachary said.

"What else then?"

"Isn't that enough?"

"I suppose so," Raymond replied, and after a pause he added, "Well, then, what do you make of it?"

Zachary vacillated for a moment, then said, "The lady, I suppose, is very attractive."

"Oh yes, she is."

"But?"

"But she's married." And there it was. He had said it, had cleared up the matter, as it were. For up to that point, his vision of what it was he was trying to get at had been blurred. But he had now, in uttering those words, made an adjustment, as if through binoculars that brought the landscape, or at least that portion of it he wished to examine, into focus. It was a bit startling to have everything that had but a few moments before been hazy suddenly appear crisply delineated. This sudden enhancement of perception did not mitigate his dilemma. His perplexity did not diminish with the increase of clarity as to its cause, but at least, he knew what he was talking about, or rather what he needed to talk about. "Do you see now what I mean?" he asked, hoping that the lucidity that had come to him had also descended on his friend.

"I see that there is more to be said," Zachary replied. For him, Raymond's words had produced the opposite effect. What he thought he understood had become less distinct. The problem had shifted from one realm to another, like suddenly finding himself above the timberline and not knowing whether he would survive in the thinner air. Again, he did not want to overstep the bounds of their friendship by broaching the matter from an angle that might embarrass his friend.

"I'm willing to talk as much as I need to, if only I knew what to say," was Raymond's retort. "Because, as you said, perplexity seems to be the hallmark of this situation."

"Is everyone else involved as perplexed as you?"

"Do you mean, is she?"

"She for one, and there is a husband."

"I can't speak for her husband. I haven't met him."

"And the lady?"

"She says that she's happy."

"Happy in her marriage?"

"Yes, happy in her marriage."

"Then, for her it's only a lark."

"It's a possibility, but I don't believe it."

"You don't believe it's just a lark?"

"I don't believe that she's happy in her marriage."

"That is a question, but is it relevant?"

"That's the crux of the matter, isn't it? Relevancy. What is relevant in all this?"

"Well, that depends, doesn't it, on what you want."

"I think it depends rather on what's possible."

"What's possible is whatever you make of it."

"That's the pragmatic view," Raymond said, "And is that the principle to act on?"

Zachary cocked his head slightly to one side as if he were taking this question more seriously than he had taken everything else. He wondered whether he had gone further than he had anticipated in drawing conclusions from the situation as he understood it. He was in fact questioning what he understood, or rather what he felt, in so far as the two were different. He felt maneuvered into a position he was not sure he wanted to be in. "I'm not advising you to act," he said, "I'm only trying to clarify what you're dealing with. I don't quite understand what the problem is, if you know what I mean."

"Oh, I know exactly what you mean," Raymond said, "And I am sorry to have made you uncomfortable. It's only that I'm in a muddle myself, and I'm clutching at straws."

"Is it only a question of her being married?"

"I don't know that it's a question of that at all."

"You mean that it's a question of her being happily married as opposed to unhappily?"

"I suppose, if you put it that way, yes."

"It's a question then of some kind of morality."

The words coming from Zachary Goodwin's mouth resonated with implications that were only dimly understood by either one of them, a sign perhaps of the changes that had occurred but were not immediately obvious. They were both aware of having crossed into a different realm.

Raymond scrutinized his friend's face, the clearly chiseled features, the pronounced eyebrows, and strong chin that was now a little soft with fatty signs of indulgence. There was also a hint of fatuousness that was borrowed from the world of successful business, which assumed that financial security translated to moral certitude. It was only a glimmer, but Raymond saw, behind the steady brown eyes, the potential for explosive growth, a change in climate that might transform a manicured park into a jungle of the unpredictable.

Raymond had a momentary longing for the simpler times, simpler in retrospect, as he remembered them, for they had seemed complicated enough when he lived through them, times when they had sat in that garden and discussed other women, or women in general, or one that had just walked by and struck them as interesting. They had specific criteria to determine what constituted an interesting woman. It had all to do with the way she looked and carried herself, for they seldom spoke to the subjects of their scrutiny, it all being an adolescent boys' pastime, and as they matured they had found their conclusions extremely dubious. It was too late now; wish as they might that it weren't, for that kind of simplicity to be serviceable.

"If you will, then, yes some kind of morality."

"What if she were unhappy? Then, it would be all right?"

"Yes, that's right, though it doesn't sound logical."

"Well, if she is unhappy that means that something is wrong already. You are not the one creating the problem."

"No, it isn't me," Raymond said.

"And that's important."

Raymond thought about that as he gazed down the garden, across the pool of water in the center, at a Maillol sculpture, a piece he had often contemplated. It was comforting to see it still there after so many years and still evoking for him a sense of elemental forces. It exhibited a truth larger than life, one for everyone to see, not to be missed even if you are befuddled by the exigencies of making intelligent decisions about everyday necessities. The sculpture spoke to him about something that was perilous to ignore. He saw the obvious allusion to the goddesses of the ancients, the essence of femininity devoid of personality, symbolic only of fecundity and of ritual sexuality. He saw the ideal form with a human face. The bronze, despite its texture, was no longer metal but the flesh of an immortal.

"Yes, of course, that's important," Raymond said.

"It's out of your hands then, isn't it?"

"I don't know about that."

"Isn't it up to her to come through?"

"To be unhappy you mean?"

"To admit it."

"Isn't that what she's doing in her own way?"

"In her own way yes, but is that enough?"

"Enough for what?"

"Enough for you to be comfortable."

"And is that a requirement?"

"That you be comfortable?"

"Yes, that I be comfortable."

"That's up to you, isn't it?"

"Well, that's what I don't know. I don't know what's up to me and what isn't."

"Well that's your problem then, not whether she's happy."

Raymond seemed not be listening, but only gazing at the sculpture of the woman, which seemed now more a mother than a siren. He wasn't far from the revelation that she could be either or both. The image soothed the discomfort in his body and in his mind, a discomfort that didn't come from the woman, but from the same source as its remedy. "Maybe it's not up to me at all," he said. "Maybe I'm just an instrument in all of this."

"As opposed to a player?"

"Yes, as opposed to a player."

"And is that better?"

"Only if it's true."

"There you are, then, right back where you started."

"Not at all," Raymond said, "Not at all." He was at that moment aware that the sculpture corresponded to something within him, something that could not have been expressed in any other way. "That sculpture moves me," he said.

"Yes, it's quite nice," Zachary Goodwin replied, "but I'm tired of sitting here."

They got up and wandered into the building, through familiar galleries, by Monet's Water Lilies and up the steps to where a helicopter hung suspended like a delicate and oversized insect. "Now there's a work of art," Zachary Goodwin said.

"It's utilitarian without being an eye sore, but is that enough?"

Zachary did not feel compelled to answer the question immediately. He merely turned it over in his mind as if it were a pebble he had just picked up on a beach and he were perusing it with his fingers to discern any variety in its texture; as if he were bringing it up to his eye and moving it away again to discover the different colors and forms that might be discerned at different distances. At the end of the examination he was satisfied that it was ordinary enough, and he tossed it to the ground where it was lost among the countless others from which it was indistinguishable.

"Well, you can't deny that it's uplifting," Zachary said.

"No, can't deny that," Raymond replied, "But it's not the same as a Maillol."

"No, it's not the same," Zachary said, "but a helicopter has a tangible effect as well as an aesthetic one."

"And for which is it displayed here, or is it for both?"

"I think only for the aesthetic, but the problem of the designer was to achieve an aesthetic effect without sacrificing function."

"Wasn't Maillol's problem the same?"

"I don't know," Zachary said, "Was it?"

This time, Raymond did not deign to answer.

# Rosamaria

*A*T AN OAK TABLE against the wall of a messy room, Rosamaria sat typing. She typed two or three words, stopped, looked straight at the wall, an expression of deep and painful thought on her face, then typed one more word and thought again. The experience had been unexpected, something to hold on to, and she was trying to get a better grasp by writing about it. Perhaps she would have a short poem by the time Hermosa arrived—yes, a short poem at the very least.

She needed something written to feel capable of coping with Hermosa—though coping was not exactly the right word. Hermosa was not forcing herself on her. She had almost begged Hermosa to drop by, but she did not feel too bad about that. What were friends for, if not to help out when needed? But Hermosa's looks made Rosamaria feel inadequate. Men were always after Hermosa, though she never had deep or lasting relationships with them. Yes, she would have the edge over Hermosa if she could get a beautiful little poem ready by the time she arrived. Rosamaria needed to regain the confidence that being married had provided. Marriage had given her leverage she had flaunted at Hermosa, as if to say, "Holding the man is what really counts." But now that her husband had left her, Rosamaria needed something else.

A row of books, among them a psychology text and three illustrated histories of the movies, rested at the edge of the cluttered table against the wall. Notebooks of various sizes comprised a pile on one side, strewn paper along with a ruler, a stapler, a jar of rubber cement, a roll of scotch tape, a cancelled bankbook, an empty roll of toilet paper, and the forked section of a twig made the rest of the table resemble a junkyard.

A Siamese cat, peering from under the bed, uttered a cry. Rosamaria looked up as the cat ambled from under the bed, jumped on the couch and onto the table. He stared at Rosamaria over the typewriter, and then wailed. Rosamaria stopped typing. The cat twisted his head slightly, the line of his eyes almost parallel to the walls. She picked him up. As she reached for him, her body moved freely in her nightgown. She was thin, her face long, her brown eyes lusterless, and her mouth too wide. The face, outlined by a thin mane of dark hair that fell timidly over her shoulders, was simultaneously comic and pathetic: the eyes, incredibly sad, the mouth, reminiscent of a clown. The red glow emanated from below the surface of her sickly complexion. As she walked into the dimly lit bedroom, she held the cat up against her breast with one hand, and with the other, she stroked his back. When she got to the bed, she put him down and lay next to him, her hand caressing his belly.

"You're all I have, Percival," she said in a languid tone. "You won't leave me, will you?" she pouted like a child. "You're beautiful, Percival, beautiful, the beautiful side of me. I'm just like you, Percival, aren't I?"

The cat raised his head and jumped to the floor. He ran into the living room towards a green armchair. He stretched his forelegs and raised his haunches. His eyes fixed on the chair, he hissed and scratched at it.

Rosamaria got up to see a man sitting there. "I hope you'll excuse the mess. I haven't been up to cleaning since I got back from the hospital," she said.

"Don't give it a second thought. I'm perfectly comfortable." He seemed an informal sort, though a tinge of vanity seeped through his deliberate shabbiness. He appeared perfectly at ease, sitting in a tattered armchair, next to a wrought iron floor lamp which Rosamaria had salvaged from the street.

The arrangement of the room was for the most part haphazard. Only the bookshelves that covered the walls flanking a non-functioning fireplace had any semblance of order. The books were not arranged in any particular sequence, but the fact that they were shelved contrasted with everything else. Cardboard boxes filled with phonograph records took up space on either side of the fireplace. The records as well as the books were half of a collection divided when Rosamaria had separated from her husband. She had kept most of the books, and he most of the records. A piece of driftwood shaped somewhat like a whale, with a knothole for an eye, was conspicuously displayed on the mantle. Rosamaria and Tom had brought it back from Cape Cod where they had spent two weeks in September the year they were married.

"Exactly what is it that you want?" Rosamaria asked.

"I want you."

"You mean you want me to sleep with you?"

The figure did not confirm or deny that but merely stared at her.

"It's a wonder you don't want Hermosa. All the men who start out after me end up wanting her."

"That's another matter," he said.

"Are you using me to get to her?"

"Certainly not," he said.

"I'm glad," she said getting up from the chair. "It's dark in here. Do you want more light?"

The man was sitting on the green armchair between the two windows. Instead of a shade, an old blanket hung over each window. The blankets were pulled aside to let in light, but in the absence of hooks, they were usually thrown over the chair to hold them back. At the moment, only one blanket was drawn, so that there was little light in the room. The man shook his head.

"You didn't come to see me at the hospital," Rosamaria said.

"I'm sorry about that. It would have been an ideal place to approach you."

"Yes, I was lonely."

"One of the reasons you went to the hospital was the desire to meet me."

"But I don't even know you," Rosamaria protested.

"For a long time you've been trying to meet up with me. Halfheartedly, I must admit, but trying nevertheless."

A look of consternation came over her face. "I don't do things halfheartedly."

"Don't you?"

She tried to be coquettish, "I don't think I like you. Go with Hermosa."

"I don't think Hermosa is ready for me."

"She'll sleep with anybody. She was engaged to be married but changed her mind when she met Ned."

"Well, that can happen to anybody."

"It happens to Hermosa all the time. Ricardo left his wife for her—broke up his marriage. Then she was unfaithful to him with Carlos."

"As I recall, you wanted Carlos for yourself."

"What if I did?"

"Well, you were still living with your husband."

"So what? He didn't want to sleep with me. When I left him, he hadn't touched me for six months."

"All that time you were seeing other men."

"How do you know that? You've been talking to somebody."

"No, I've been watching you for a long time."

"I never noticed you." She was only mildly curious about that. "Anyway I'm glad you like me better than Hermosa. She's always trying to take men away from me. She doesn't even have to try. When they see her, they want her. Sometimes she gets alarmed at her own sensuality."

"Perhaps her therapist admonishes her."

"Yes, but she can't stop. She's always happy to pick up her skirt and have the lace of her underwear admired."

"And you're not like that?"

"I'm not."

"Didn't you just have an abortion? The guy who knocked you up hasn't even come to see you since you went to the hospital, has he?"

She had been preparing for that one and did not flinch. "That doesn't prove anything."

"No, it doesn't. But you've been after me for so long."

"I haven't. You're crazy."

"In any case, it's time for us to be together." He stood up looking at her intently.

"Are you going to take me by force?"

"I won't have to, will I?"

Just then, the doorbell rang. Rosamaria turned her back on the stranger, glad not to have to speak to him any longer. The living room opened directly onto the bedroom. The only hints of a physical divider were two closets that jutted from opposing walls at the point where one room became another. The bedroom was dark. The glass on the only window, facing an air shaft, had been painted. The double bed was unmade, and near the pillow rested a box of Kleenex tissues. Next to the bed stood a night table; on it rested an assortment of pill bottles, a pad of paper, and a shaded lamp. She walked through the bedroom and into the kitchen to get to the door.

It was Hermosa. She always had, like a permanent infirmity incurred in an accident, a constrained smile on her lips. As soon as she walked in, she sat down at the round dining table, and Rosamaria offered her tea.

"Okay, but I have to leave soon. I came to see if you needed anything."

"I'm glad you came," Rosamaria said.

She walked to the sink to get a pot for the tea. The small kitchen sink was next to the bathtub, and dirty dishes overflowed into the tub. On the opposite side, by the door to the next room, the kitty litter in the cat box had been overused. A large straw mat, rigged over the window at the end of the room, was lowered at the moment, and under the window, against the radiator, rested four paper bags replete with garbage.

While Rosamaria served the tea, the cat ambled under the table.

"Will you get this cat away from me!" Hermosa said, pushing the cat away with her foot.

"He won't hurt you," Rosamaria said.

"He ripped my stocking."

"He never attacks anybody else." Then overwhelmed by the lie, "He senses you don't like him."

"That's not so. Let's drink the tea in the other room. I can't stand the smell in here."

"You're always criticizing me," on the verge of tears, "God! You're supposed to be my friend! Stop criticizing me!"

"I didn't mean to criticize. Doesn't the smell bother you?"

"I don't smell anything!" She picked up her cup and started for the living room.

A phosphorescent poster hung on one wall of the small room adjacent to the kitchen. From the center of the red background emanated an exotic motif that resembled Arabic writing creating a circle. Hermosa examined it.

"I got it from a witch at the hospital," Rosamaria said. "She invited me to a séance."

Hermosa looked at Rosamaria blankly.

"After the experience I had while under ether… I can't describe it. I simply made contact with something beyond, something in another world. But how can I expect you to understand?" Then catching herself, "I don't mean anything. Only that it's hard to explain to someone who hasn't had the experience." She had not been able to write anything, so she decided she would not mention the experience again. Once in the living room they both sat on the couch.

"I met Susan Greerson in the subway," Hermosa said.

Rosamaria grimaced.

"She doesn't like you either."

"Oh well, it was her fault—telling everyone I was already twenty-nine."

"You told me you're twenty-nine."

"I didn't tell you that! How could I tell you that?"

She got to her feet, the red under her skin pulsating. She looked like something viewed under a microscope: a fluid always on the verge of losing its boundaries. "I'm only twenty-two. I'll show you my birth certificate." She rushed to the dresser in the bedroom, opened a drawer and making a great deal of noise began a frantic search. The room was dark, and she was not altogether visible from the living room. After a while she said, "Well, I don't have a birth certificate." She breathed hard, as if she were asthmatic.

"You ought to get one."

Rosamaria sat on the bed, one hand on her chest. "I can't because there isn't one," she said raising her head and looking straight at Hermosa who sat still.

"Everyone has a birth certificate," Hermosa said.

"Well, I don't, and I don't want to talk about it. I want to talk about something else. Will you do me a favor and go with me to see Tom? I want to ask him for some money."

"I don't think I should," Hermosa replied.

"I'm not well yet," Rosamaria argued. "The trip might be too much. What if I faint or something?"

"Call him up and ask him to bring it."

"He won't. You know him."

"I know him. That's why I'm not going."

"I'll have to ask my father for the money," Rosamaria said.

"You told me your father was dead."

"I mean my stepfather. I don't know my father. I don't know if he's dead or not."

"You told me he was."

"I don't know! I don't know! Stop torturing me!"

"Well, I was about to leave anyway."

"No, no, what are you getting upset for? Don't go."

"I have to leave now," Hermosa said finishing her tea.

"Don't go yet."

"Really, I have to go. I have so much to do."

"Please, stay a little longer."

"I can't, really. I just came to see if you were all right."

After Hermosa left, Rosamaria locked the door and waited to hear Hermosa's footsteps as she descended the stairs. The neighbor's dog on the floor below barked as Hermosa went by, but even then, Rosamaria did not move but stared at the green door, which was divided into four recessed rectangles with molding on each side. The two rectangles in the upper part were longer than the two in the lower. The lock's copper color had been worn away around the knob, revealing the black metal. Four screws held the lock to the door. The remnant of a door chain hung below the lock, and beneath that, missing its knob, an old fashion lock that had been superseded by the copper color one. Above the working lock there was a handle for pulling the door open. All these items, except the working lock, but including the large hinges, were painted green like the rest of the door.

As Rosamaria walked back into the bedroom, she noticed the figure sitting in the tattered armchair. Rosamaria could not make out the face of the figure wearing a gray robe, the cowl of which cast a shadow on his face. His head turned slightly towards the oak table, the figure sat perfectly still. Silently, Rosamaria lay on the bed and stared at the ceiling. After a while, she turned her eyes towards the tattered armchair. Now, the figure was standing, his robe hanging loosely in folds, his face still masked by shadow. Rosamaria silently gazed at him; then she looked towards the table on which rested a shaded lamp, a pad of paper, and an assortment of pill bottles.

She reached for one of the bottles, read the label to make sure it was the right one. She unscrewed the top and poured half the content into the palm of her right hand. The figure moved through the bedroom but did not stop at the bed. Rosamaria's eyes followed him. Hermosa was now standing by the doorway of the bedroom, the figure unzipping her dress. Rosamaria turned her head so as not to watch. A smile disfigured her face as she poured the pills back into the bottle.

# The Desk

*I*T *HAD BEEN* Cynthia's idea to meet for lunch. She was periodically possessed by the notion that she must take better care of her mother, whom she often imagined languishing in her Upper West Side apartment not knowing what to do with herself. It was a fantasy gratifying to the daughter who would at those moments fling herself into the task of teaching her mother, Mrs. Margo Adler, how to avoid boredom, which Cynthia imagined was her mother's most serious challenge.

These moods were genuine but conveniently fleeting. There were times when Cynthia took up residence in other cities in order to experience a variety of urban settings. She thought such excursions necessary to achieve the complete absorption of American culture. On those occasions, her mother's plight didn't seem so onerous, and she hardly thought of her mother as needing any assistance.

When she was away, she occasionally wondered whether her mother was lonely, but the kind of loneliness that Cynthia associated with her mother was not easily fixed with superficial distractions. Its inevitability kept Cynthia from thinking about it more often, but her good nature kept her from ignoring it when close by and in the mood to be charitable. Without reservation she blamed her father for her mother's misery, but as he was impervious to criticism from her, or anyone else, she confined her efforts to attempting to bring about a change in her mother's outlook. At the moment she was engaged in defending herself from her mother who was taking her to task, if ever so gently, for having put Henry, as she put it, in harm's way. Henry was one of Cynthia's friends; with whom the senior Adlers had both formed an attachment, and who had recently gone through a divorce.

"Well," Cynthia said, "he's a big boy, and he's perfectly capable of looking out for himself."

"He is, after all, just like one of our own," Mrs. Adler continued unnecessarily explaining her concern.

"Yes, of course. That's why I'm so desperately trying to help him," Cynthia said.

"I'm completely amazed at what you consider help," Mrs. Adler went on.

"I think you underestimate his ability to cope," Cynthia insisted.

"One can never underestimate a man's ability to take care of himself."

"At any rate we'll be close by to rescue him, if the need arises."

"That I think is taking unnecessary chances. An ounce of prevention..."

"What in the world do you want to prevent?" Cynthia ventured, knowing that her mother would not dare to reveal the true reason for her displeasure.

"I would like to prevent his having any more trouble than he already has. It's bad enough what happened with Gail."

"Yes, it was bad enough," Cynthia agreed. "But it's not our fault."

"I'm not interested in attributing fault. I only wish to avoid another mistake."

"Yes, but we are not the ones that have to avoid it."

"We shouldn't be the ones to promote it either." That was the least Mrs. Adler could say at the moment without being misunderstood by her daughter.

The situation was delicate, but Mrs. Adler was uncertain of just how delicate it was. She had to be careful not to ruin anything that might be going her way. She did have a very definite idea of which way she wanted events to proceed, but she was uncertain of whether she would, at the rate she was going, ever get to her destination. Indeed, she felt she was in a strong current, paddling in the opposite direction, and it was all she could do to stay in place. She would have gladly stayed in place for the moment, just so long as she did not get pushed back any further, though when she thought about it, she did not see how much further back she could be pushed. Unless it was to the point where Cynthia would be married, and there would be no hope at all of un-marrying her. Of course, a situation with no hope at all would be far-fetched since as she had discovered, marriage did not have to be, contrary to a prevailing rumor, forever. But that was not the preferred scenario. Divorce, though not always messy, was never elegant; and Mrs. Adler would have liked to spare Cynthia an inelegant episode in her life if she could.

"You know," Cynthia said, "We don't have to solve Henry's problems over lunch."

Mrs. Adler could not agree more as they sat eating their cucumber salad by the restaurant window looking out on Fifth Avenue. Mrs. Adler knew better than Cynthia how well Henry would take care of himself, but it served her purpose to let Cynthia think that her concern for Henry was paramount. Certainly it was better that she think her concern was over Henry than over Cynthia herself.

"Perhaps you are right," Mrs. Adler said, "no sense wasting a beautiful day worrying about what one can't do anything about."

It was the right tack to take for the moment since she could take no other, and she was almost certain that Cynthia didn't detect any dissimilitude. It wasn't easy, however, to determine what Cynthia was hatching behind her insouciant smile. For it occurred to Mrs. Adler that her daughter was pushing concern away from Henry just as subtly as Mrs. Adler herself was pushing in the other direction, and that gave her pause to think that there was more to her daughter's nonchalance than was obvious.

This twist created a momentary alarm, for she could think of no reason why Cynthia would be steering her away from the subject, except to save her from some greater disappointment about Henry's condition. As she had exaggerated what she was feeling, Cynthia might be trying to keep from her something truly horrendous.

Her panic was brief, as she reasoned that Cynthia herself would not be so calm if Henry were really in trouble. She was, nevertheless, alerted to something not to be ignored, and as she thought it futile to confront Cynthia directly with her suspicions, she decided to bide her time. She had all day to delve to the bottom of the mystery. The time limit did not indicate a point at which she would abandon her efforts to discover what Cynthia was hiding. It was only an estimate of how long it might take.

There would be enough distraction during the day to put either one of them off guard, and Mrs. Adler was determined not to be the one who would lose sight of her purpose. Even the weather was conspiring to lead them astray from any endeavor except that of relaxation. It was a mild spring day. The air promised wonderful things to come, an enticing promise despite past experience of it always resulting in a sweltering summer. But it had yet to arrive, and the bitter cold of winter, which lingered more and more into March and even April, was surely gone. Being between two unpleasant extremes was perhaps what gave the season, over and above the promise of renewal, its special character, that golden mean which the philosopher had named the aim of all virtuous life.

Mrs. Adler was not searching for new beginnings for herself, but she would not stint her efforts on behalf of those close to her, for whom it was not yet too late. It was not too late for Cynthia or Henry though they were, surprisingly, the ones most bent on self-destruction. This point of view, she knew, was not held by all. And perhaps it was held only by her, though she suspected that there were others capable of a clear vision. After all, Henry had a mother who surely was just as concerned over him. If two mothers could put their heads together they might hatch a plan to put their children on the right path, but as desirable as that idea seemed to her at the moment, she knew there was little hope of putting it into practice.

She was not on such terms with Mrs. Riffman that she might call her with schemes about her son. Beside, Mrs. Riffman was off in Florida basking in her retirement, and might from such a distance not be completely apprised of what was going on. It would be difficult to explain; with the chance that Mrs. Adler's interest might come across as a little bizarre. As much as she would have liked an ally, it was preferable just then to go at it alone. At the moment, she had to deal with Cynthia, and there was no hope of assistance from anyone. She was thrown back on her own wits, and where her children were concerned, they had in the past luckily not let her down.

So, as they walked down Bleecker Street after lunch looking in the windows of the antique shops, she was set ostensibly in the market for a small desk, a secretary she could keep in the sewing room, her favorite space. She spent so much time there, but it had no proper desk at which to work, with drawers for her papers and writing implements and postal paraphernalia, and for her diary which deserved a special place of its own.

She had all those things in the library now, but she had never really liked the library. It was too big and too formal, and she had never meant to keep it as a work-space for herself. It had been meant for Paul. But of course he never used it when they lived together, if one could say that they ever lived together. Her husband had seldom been home, even at the beginning when he pretended to love her. It rankled her still, after so many years, that it had been all a sham. Though he would claim even now that it wasn't so—that he had been devoted to her all along, that those other women had meant nothing, and that it had been she who had driven him away with unreasonable jealousy. He discounted all the years of her silent suffering, all the years of her looking the other way because she saw no way of remedying the situation, and because in the back of her mind, it was scarcely noticeable. Nevertheless, still there to be glimpsed lurked the gnawing regret that she might be to blame; if not completely, at least in part because she was still, albeit secretly, in love with someone else.

At the beginning of her marriage, she had feared that the secret could not be kept. The fact might not be revealed, but the effect of it perhaps could not be avoided, and it was conceivable that Paul felt a holding back on her part; a keeping to herself of that little place, small as it was, where the memory of her first true love persisted. It was, she later concluded, an ungrounded fear. Even if he had been interested in observing her that closely, Paul lacked that power of insight. She had the right to a private memory, and it did not detract from her devotion to her marriage. But as it turned out, that became irrelevant, because Paul was from the beginning beyond redemption. It wasn't the other women that mattered; even had there been no other women, he would not have been more attentive and would not have loved her in the ways she wanted. He had a character flaw beyond repair. She had tried and failed, and her failure had resulted in guilt.

Cynthia saw that her mother was upset about something, but she thought it only a nervousness that afflicted Mrs. Adler when she faced the prospect of spending a large sum of money, which the price of an antique represented, relative to what she might get from another sort of vendor. Being a thoroughly modern young lady Cynthia had no doubt that the remedy for having a bee in one's bonnet was taking off the bonnet, and so she had no scruples against helping her mother do just that by suggesting that money wasn't everything. Mrs. Adler could not agree more with the statement. Especially since she had not connected it to her current activity, which was very likely to culminate in the outflow of a tidy amount.

"After a point money doesn't matter much," Mrs. Adler said.

Cynthia was gratified that her mother was so readily open to that thought just at the moment when they came to a shop window that promised both the possibility of their finding just the item that would go well in the sewing room and the certainty that the price would be commensurate with the gratification derived from the object.

"Whatever you spend will be well worth the money," Cynthia said.

Mrs. Adler made a face that Cynthia could only interpret as her mother's avowed indifference to the amount that might presently change hands.

"What, then, are you worried about?" Cynthia blurted in a momentary lapse of restraint.

"Do I look worried?" her mother asked.

The question was disingenuous, and it dawned on Cynthia that her mother had not let go of the subject that had come up earlier in their conversation. Cynthia was not indifferent to her mother's wishes. She sincerely wanted to spare her mother as much grief as was consistent with her own agenda, which if Mrs. Adler would but analyze carefully, did not deviate much from her own. It was difficult, however, for Cynthia to get this across to her mother without telling her more than she wanted to reveal. She did not want to be secretive at all, if she could help it, but she also did not want to falsely elevate her mother's hopes.

At the moment, Cynthia saw that she had to make an appeal for a clear sign that everything was all right. The need for reassurance surprised her, for she had thought that in this matter, at the very least, she had gone beyond parental dependency. It made her wonder what in fact the "everything" was that needed to be all right, and whether the very asking of the question was an indication that everything was not all right.

They walked into the shop, and from the back, the proprietor raised his eyes from a ledger to look them over and make an accurate assessment of what sort of customers they were. He exhibited his conclusion by not immediately rising from his seat to their assistance. He saw that they might have a very definite idea of what they wanted, but would pretend to be open-minded as they looked around, and so he gave them the opportunity to do so. It wasn't long before just the thing they were looking for was discovered, as it was inevitable that something that was on display should be. But it was perhaps the art of the dealer to arrange his wares in such a manner as to give his customers the feeling of having unearthed their find; having done so, of course, without the inconvenience of actually moving dirt or having to clear it off the object. This was indeed why he felt justified after having had the item rediscovered in his very own shop, in charging a premium that might seem exorbitant to one who did not understand the process.

Mother and daughter were looking at a drop leaf desk that had been manufactured in Pennsylvania in the late eighteenth century. It looked appropriately brittle for a wooden object of such age and had a characteristic crack along the grain on one side, which had been fashioned from one wide board. The wood had acquired a golden glow from repeated application of linseed oil which, however, magnified every dent and scratch the desk had acquired during its centuries of service.

Cynthia discreetly inspected the tag that hung from one of the draw pulls to prepare herself for her mother's inevitable reaction because despite of Mrs. Adler's indications to the contrary, Cynthia expected the usual reluctance to purchase an expensive item that was not an absolute necessity. The tag indicated a price greater than Cynthia had guessed, although she was apt on most occasions to spend more than she had to, if only to differ from her mother. But she was undisturbed by the discovery, knowing full well that Mrs. Adler's reluctance in this area bore no relation to her financial condition. Extravagance in instances of this sort made no material difference to Mrs. Adler. Cynthia did not immediately announce what she had discovered from the tag, a sign that Mrs. Adler correctly interpreted to mean that Cynthia was trying to keep from her an unpleasant fact. Mrs. Adler, however, was determined to show her daughter that she could transcend old habits, and that she would evaluate the desk purely on grounds of utility and aesthetics without even looking at the price tag, which she proceeded to pretend did not exist.

"All I have to consider is whether this is really what I want," Mrs. Adler said.

"Yes, that's what you must consider."

"And also if it's what I need," Mrs. Adler continued.

"Isn't that the same thing?" Cynthia inquired rhetorically, thinking that the answer had to be in the affirmative.

"Well, not at all," Mrs. Adler said. "What I want can be influenced by some surface quality that excites the imagination. One can fall in love with an image whereas what one needs has to be serviceable. I have to be able to sit down and write at a desk, not just have it for show. It's an important distinction."

"What I mean is that very often wanting something is an indication of a need not necessarily recognized."

"I need a desk," Mrs. Adler said, "I don't necessarily need this particular one."

"I'm saying that you might need something to write on that's also old and beautiful and has a character acquired over a long period of time. The old and beautiful part is a need also."

"Perhaps you're right," Mrs. Adler said, though she only vaguely understood what Cynthia meant, and was more intent on making herself understood.

This exchange was followed by silence at which point Cynthia might have interjected the price of the desk, but she refrained, thinking to let her mother's plan unfold and clearly indicate what she was up to. She had a distinct sense that she was dealing with something unavoidable.

"I don't think this is what I want," Mrs. Adler said, "It's too precious, too delicate. Beside it's the first thing we've seen. I think I should look at more items before I decide."

"There's no logical reason why the first thing you look at shouldn't be the right one."

"No, no logical reason," Mrs. Adler conceded, "but logic is not a consideration here, is it? I just have to feel that it's right."

"And does that method always work for you?" Cynthia inquired.

"It works often enough," Mrs. Adler replied.

This was enough to give Cynthia pause to ponder what it was that her mother was trying to convey in so elaborate a manner. It was a question now of whether it was furniture that Mrs. Adler was trying to buy or whether that was only a move in a more complex game.

"You don't have to settle for this one," Cynthia said. "You can always come back if you don't find anything better."

"Unless of course he sells it to somebody else in the meantime," Mrs. Adler pondered.

"Not much likelihood of that," Cynthia said, "I think this is not the kind of object that moves very fast."

"You never can tell what's going to go and what isn't," Mrs. Adler said.

"Well, if you're afraid to lose it, grab it now," Cynthia said.

"If I were afraid to lose it, I would," Mrs. Adler said.

The shopkeeper, with an uncanny sense of when to make his move, decided at that point to approach them, though he had been sitting too far away to hear their conversation. He walked up to them with an air of authority, natural enough since it was his establishment. But his purpose, he gave out, was to congratulate them on their good taste. It was obvious to him that the younger woman was more taken with the antique desk than was the older one, but that it was the older one who was shopping. He would have preferred that it was the other way around, because the younger woman he rightly assessed was not as particular about parting with money, not ever having known the want of it. They were not collectors, he knew; the value of the object to them was more to give accent to the decor of a room than to appreciate monetarily over time, or to satisfy a passion for the old. His customers were of all ilks; the effect for him was the same, but each type had to be handled differently.

"You can't find a finer piece of furniture than this," the dealer said.

"For a museum perhaps," Mrs. Adler responded, "but I need something serviceable. This may be a little too brittle for constant use."

"On the contrary. This piece has withstood the test of time. It has been in use for two hundred years, and it can easily withstand another two hundred. It was made to last. Construction like this is unknown today." He pulled out the top drawer to point out the dovetailing. "Moreover," he continued, "it has already weathered as much as it's going to, so you don't have to worry about anymore splits and cracks. In the old days when they could still find trees big enough they made the sides from one board, so there was more give and take as the wood aged, causing cracks as you can see right here on the side. But all the aging has happened already. You don't have to worry about that anymore."

He gambled that they were not familiar enough with the technique of furniture construction to know why the side of the desk had split, so would not object to his half-truth explanation. He was right in his assessment of their technical knowledge, but he did not count on Mrs. Adler's intuitive sense that she was not hearing the complete story. She had no idea what that might be, but certainly not what she was getting, and it came upon her suddenly that she was tired of dealing with such petty deceptions. She was especially incensed that this shopkeeper should presume to lie to her when there was really no need. The object that he was trying to sell was eloquent enough on its own behalf.

"Really," she said, "I think old things are more apt to crack than new ones, and something that has cracked in the past is more apt to crack in the future. Really, you take me for a young girl, do you?"

The outburst was quite spontaneous, and it was the one reaction neither the shopkeeper nor Cynthia expected. The shopkeeper felt compelled to deal with it, while Cynthia took the opportunity to study the phenomenon, if only to protect herself from a similar one in the future.

"Perhaps this is not the piece for you," the shopkeeper said. He was a tall man with a bald head, and he now took on an air of offended dignity. "One must be comfortable with a purchase, otherwise there is no enjoyment; and that, after all, is what it's all about."

Mrs. Adler realized that she had not meant to go as far as that—that she had needed only a *bon mot* to have achieved her purpose with much more finesse, but it was the purpose which had gotten away from her. She did not in truth want to pick a fight with a shopkeeper, especially not about a piece of second hand furniture, no matter that it was two hundred years old and Benjamin Franklin might have used it while writing letters to his mistress. Mrs. Adler would have never suspected, when she was growing up, that the most avuncular of founding fathers, her favorite, had been a philanderer. But what did that matter? It wasn't the shopkeeper's fault, and perhaps this wasn't even Benjamin Franklin's desk, even if was manufactured in Philadelphia just about the time he would have had the opportunity to purchase it. What had Benjamin Franklin to do with Cynthia anyway? He might have been still philandering when he was an old man, but so what? He was dead now and Cynthia could go off and marry

Alexander Hamilton and become a young widow. Young people did not know how to avoid the pitfalls. What was a mother to do?

"Maybe there is something else you can show me," she said by way of appeasement.

Of course there was something else to show. There was always something else, and he tried to entice back his good cheer, because his livelihood, after all, depended on it. There was something else, but not quite as spectacular as the first one, and the ladies were disappointed as he had suspected they would be. There was nothing else in the shop that took their fancy. They were about to leave, when he remembered that he did have another desk that had not yet been prepared for display. He meant to have it refinished before he brought it down to the floor, but if they cared to see it as it was he would be glad to take them upstairs, where the unfinished pieces were stored. There was nothing to be lost except time, they felt, in these days of no scarcity. So they followed him with a heightened sense of adventure, as if they were leaving the commercial establishment altogether and entering an enchanted attic where the past waited patiently dormant to be coaxed into the present.

Mrs. Adler had no expectation of finding anything appropriate for her purposes, but she was in the spirit of the search, and she was willing to follow her nose, which at the moment was following the shopkeeper. Cynthia didn't care much one way or another, but she saw that her mother was content and that was enough for her to happily tramp up the stairs to the dusty storage room, replete with furniture stacked up to the ceiling. The narrowest of passageways afforded access. The shopkeeper moved several pieces, with no small amount of trouble as it was not easy to find room to shift the objects, but he managed dexterously enough, though his efforts in the end were in vain.

The desk that he uncovered met the requirement of being sturdy enough for everyday use, but it lacked the charm of the one they had seen downstairs. It was not as old or as quaint, though quaintness was not what they had asked for. What it offered was serviceable oak construction, in a plain nineteenth century style. It was, in a word, a disappointment, which registered without restraint on Mrs. Adler's face. It was perhaps to escape that look, which she took as a reproach, that Cynthia walked to the end of the passageway to peer around the corner into a relatively uncluttered area at the center of which she saw something she had not expected. She beckoned to her mother to come see, and Mrs. Adler dutifully complied, glad enough to get away from the hideous apparition of utilitarianism.

Cynthia had stumbled upon a workspace in which pieces were prepared before they were brought down to the shop for display. What had attracted her attention was a secretary with cabriole legs. This was what was generally considered a lady's desk, but that was not what had caught her attention but the fact that this one was ornately decorated with wood inlaid. The decoration went beyond the usual geometric designs and broke out into floral patterns along the edges with fully articulated rustic scenes in the center of all the major panels. The writing surface was a plain mahogany that provided a welcome relief from the bustle of the rest of the piece.

Mrs. Adler's jaw froze in an open position when she saw the desk, and it was a few moments before she regained her presence of mind to say, "That's the one I want."

The shopkeeper took on the air of an undertaker who, meeting the members of the bereaved family for the first time, wants to make no mistake about conveying how much he understands their sorrow. His expression communicated the full extent of the problem before he had the opportunity to utter a word. It came as no surprise, when he said, "That piece has been sold."

The words made no impression on Mrs. Adler, who, the moment she surmised their coming had begun trying to discover some way to contravene the reality they represented. She was busy thinking of how she might prevail on any of the parties involved to annul whatever contract existed, but she could not come up with any legal or moral solution to the conundrum, especially since she was only in the presence of the seller who was bound inextricably to his end of the contract. The shopkeeper interpreted her silence as a sign of deep disappointment. Not suspecting the machination of the lady's active imagination and with a misguided sense of kindness, he began to relate the details of the sale that had brought her to her immediate state of grief in the mistaken belief that knowing that she had come close to acquiring what she desired would make her feel better.

"It was just yesterday that I sold it," he said, "to a young man who I think intends it as a present for his intended."

"I'm sure he can get her something more practical," Mrs. Adler said, "Like a diamond bracelet. Perhaps I can do business with him," she continued. "If you would care to tell me how I can get in touch with him, I would be glad to make him an offer worth his while, and of course I would be glad also to pay you a commission for the service."

Being a man of business the shopkeeper didn't see this as a totally outrageous proposition, although he was surprised at the lady's vehement attachment to an object that she had but laid eyes on a few minutes before. "It wouldn't be ethical of me to give out information about a customer without his permission, but if you leave me a number at which you can be reached, I will pass on your offer, and he can call you if he is interested."

Having concluded that piece of the business, mother and daughter left the shop. Out in the street Cynthia expressed her wonderment at how her mother had handled the situation. She had never before seen her mother be so aggressive and forthright.

"Mom, you did that wonderfully," Cynthia repeated.

"In my old age," Mrs. Adler said, "I have at long last learned how to get what I want."

Cynthia took that in as something to be reckoned with. As they continued their amble down Bleecker Street, she had an uncomfortable sense of having to reconsider what she could expect from her mother.

# The Call

"*GO RIGHT AHEAD,* call," she said.

Ricardo hesitated. He extended his hand until the tip of his fingers touched the telephone, and then made a gesture as if to remove the dust from the black instrument. He would feel more at ease with a different color telephone, green for instance. A green telephone would certainly be more pleasant and evoke more confidence in him; black telephones were so businesslike and black such an ominous color—hard to be successful when even the color of the instrument works against you. But he couldn't bring himself to tell her that.

She stood staring into the street from a window of the apartment, though there was nothing in the street that called for fixed attention. A slight gust of wind created eddies of debris along the curb. The small waves of dust rose, each in a gentle arc that tapered off at the ends and then collapsed, the individual grains of earth disappearing on the rough surface of the pavement. The streetlights had come on to illuminate the joint performance of the wind and the dust.

"It's better to do it in person," he finally said.

He gathered from her grimace that no help was forthcoming. The possibility of being mistaken about the woman standing across the room assaulted him, but the will to walk out failed to emerge. There was still the hope that everything was a misunderstanding, that somehow he had lost his footing, but that soon everything would be back to normal. If he persisted, he might stumble upon the correct words or the appropriate gesture. Everything would then magically fall into place, and she would be what she had seemed when they first met.

"I'm going to do it in person," he insisted. "It's better that way."

"Oh?"

The question was precise. It was elegant. It had the sleekness of crafted metal, as if out of stainless steel a sculptor had created that "Oh?" or a painter had depicted it in the coldest blue, with a base of ochre to suggest a glimmering desire to escape from a monotonous completeness of such a question. It was characteristic of her style. She took on the guise of that rhetorical device; she was a question that included an unequivocal answer.

He suppressed his anger, and he groped for an appropriate manifestation of what ought to have been. Observing him, she walked to the small table where her handbag lay, and she took out a cigarette. She struck the match several times before it lit. She then sat down in a plush upholstered chair, put the bag on her lap and gazed at it intently.

"This is a nice bag. It was thoughtful of you to buy it for me."

In desperation, Ricardo turned his eyes toward the ceiling.

"It was," she continued, "thoughtful of you. This bag has character."

"And I don't. Is that it?"

"I didn't say that."

"You think you're sharp!"

"I'm not trying to be sharp, Ricardo. I'm trying to be helpful." She added, "Forget the phone call."

"I'm going to call," he insisted, trying to be forceful.

"Forget it," she persisted. "Do it in person."

He again put his hand on the receiver but stopped. What would he say? What if the words didn't come to him? He would make a fool of himself. He picked up the phone and began to dial while trying to formulate what to say. He let it ring; no one answered. He let the phone ring five times, and then hung up.

"No one answered," he said.

"You dialed the wrong number."

In his head, a bottle of ink tipped over and the black liquid seeped through his mind. He looked at her incredulously. He ceased to deal with incoming impressions and concentrated on coping with the internal crisis. He tried to focus on a specific object in order to allay his anguish, but just as it would have been impossible for him to refrain from screaming had he incurred a physical injury, he was unable to avert the consequences of an abstract blow. He focused only on the pain centered in his mind and diffusing through his body.

She relentlessly continued. "Are you going to dial the right number or not?"

Automatically, he picked up the phone and again began to dial, but suddenly he slammed the receiver and sank into a chair. He hated her. He wanted to scream and curse at her, but even that was muffled. Perplexity overwhelmed him. "What's with you?" he moaned. "What's with you?"

# Sale at Barney's

*W*ALKING THROUGH THE living room to get to the door, Pacheco smiled at the old woman who, staring at the silent television, sat on the sofa, images flowing as she improvised the sound track. For an instant, her gaze turned from the screen—he merely a shadow distracting her.

"*Abuela, te veo,*" he said, gliding across the room as if he were in a ballroom. "Shit, when are you going to learn English?" he said still smiling, knowing full well that she didn't understand a word.

Down in the street, he walked with a light step, until he ran into Hector.

"Hey, Pacheco, you're all dressed up," Hector said. "Where're you headed?"

"Just down the block," Pacheco replied swinging his shoulders.

"Man, they've been looking for you," Hector said.

"Who?"

"The guys, that's who."

"Well, everybody knows where I live," Pacheco said.

"Damn it, you're all dressed up," Hector repeated.

"What about Tony? You seen Tony?"

"Ain't seen'm today," Hector said.

"Damn it, I need to see'm."

"You dressed up to see Tony?"

"Shit, I ain't dressed up."

"You look dressed up. Going to impress your woman, ain't you?"

"Hey, think about something else," he said.

He had to see Tony, but Tony wasn't answering his calls. Of course, he could be home and not answer the phone, but that was very unlikely. What kind of a guy wouldn't answer the phone? And in any case, his woman would answer the phone and take a message, but nobody was answering the phone. He had the right number. He had looked it up in the phone book, and then he had called information to double check. He did have the right number, but still he was getting no answer. Shit, where could Tony be? He had to find Tony before Tony's guys came around, any time now. He had waited too long. No, that wasn't really what happened. He hadn't waited for anything. Waiting means you know you have to do something, but you don't do it. But this whole thing just came on, developed on its own, before he had time to think.

"Hey, do me a favor," he said to Hector, "go around and try to find Tony. Tell'm I've gotta see him."

"Shit, I don't know where he is."

"Well, if you see'm tell'm I'll be at the Farango Club."

"Sure," Hector said, "I'll tell'm." And having lost interest in what Pacheco had to say, he sauntered away.

"Shit, he's a nutcase," Pacheco murmured. Even if Hector ran into Tony, he wouldn't remember to convey the message. Couldn't depend on Hector, but then there really wasn't anyone at all one could depend on. At the moment all on his own, Pacheco had to find Tony.

"Yo, Pacheco!" a voice assailed him from the street.

Shit, man, what now? Last thing in the world he needed at the moment was to see this guy.

A black Chevrolet had pulled over to the curb by the fire hydrant, the driver's taut face disfigured by a forced smile. His teeth seemed to struggle to escape from a prison flooded with odorous saliva. He was not a young man, rather someone on the verge of crossing the demarcation that would forever bar him from that description but at the moment struggling to keep from stepping over. He resembled a fugitive on the run from time, and in the process disguised in a black leather jacket, a silver chain around his neck along with an ostentatious gold ring on one of the fingers of his right hand.

"Get in," the guy in the car said to Pacheco.

"Shit, man, not here," Pacheco responded, looking around to check whether anyone was watching.

"Down at the place then," the man said, "right now." The Chevy pulled out and sped down the street.

Okay, the guy wasn't playing the game by the rules, but there was no simple way out of the predicament. Something was rising inside of Pacheco, a vine spreading, entangling his inner organs and squeezing them. He felt it growing from the bottom of his stomach. If it got to his lungs, expanding and contracting would stop, and once at his heart, the beating would cease. He had to get rid of it altogether; or at least keep it in his stomach. Of course, that had its own problems. He had to get a hold of himself. There had to be a way out. He didn't see it just yet, but it would come to him. He had to believe in himself, in luck, in something! Stay calm, cool and collected. That was the trick, and he was good at it. He had been until now, at least, and there was no reason yet to panic.

Detective Rosario was a fuck. That's all there was to it. Easy to say now, but there must've been a reason why dealing with him had seemed desirable at some point. Well, there was the money of course. That was something. Can't dress well without money; that's for sure. Pacheco stopped to contemplate his reflection in the window of a parked car. Shit, he did look good, the money well spent. You can't go through life looking like shit. You have to make yourself look like what you want to be, and eventually you physically become what you imagine. What else is there? Only a very slight difference between pretense and reality, and then one becomes the other. He headed toward the Farango Club.

The first blow landed on the side of his head, and the next right above the stomach, between the ribs. Bent over, he reeled. "Shit, man, what's up?" he managed to say before the next blow caused him to stagger.

"You tell me."

Tony's voice, he could tell, though he couldn't really see the face staying in the shadows, on purpose no doubt. "I've been looking for you," Pacheco said, raising his hand to shade his eyes from the light of the street lamp. If he could only see Tony's face, he would be able to arrive at a more precise assessment of his immediate predicament. Tony's eyes would reveal exactly how far he intended to go, and that was all Pacheco wanted to know at the moment, all he needed to know. No matter what he saw, he had to act as if there were a way out, at least with his life, even at the price of few broken bones. That, after all, would be a bargain, like a sale at Barney's. Shit, one ran the risk of being trampled at the door on sale day when a thousand dollar suit could go for merely five hundred bucks.

"They say you've been talking," Tony said.

"Shit, man, you don't believe that, do you? And anyway, what could I say? I know nothing. Isn't that right? And besides, you're my cousin, right? Why would I ever say anything about you? *Abuela* would kill me."

"Should I save her the trouble?"

"Shit, Tony, don't fool around. I'm serious."

"Let this be a lesson."

The sound of the approaching siren undulated from the distance. Tony's companions quickly moved in, beat Pacheco to the ground, and kicked him as if he were a feather pillow. Instinctively, he curled himself into a small bundle, arms crossed over his head. About to pass out, he thought, "Shit man, they're ruining my suit."

# Thursday Night

*I*N *AUTUMN HIS* body became sensitized. The change of weather affected his health, and throughout the season he ran a slight fever. At dusk, the street appeared deserted except for the stern façades of the buildings on either side. The cold wind chilled his skin, while underneath, the blood circulated feverishly. Light shone from some of the windows, and from some, shadows darted grotesquely mimicking their source. Roberto turned left when he reached the corner of Twentieth and Seventh. He glanced down the street, and then looked at the ground directly before him, a long walk from the corner to Anna's place.

The wind blew eddies of debris along the curbs. The streetlights had come on to illuminate the joint performance of the wind and the dust. He zipped up his jacket and put his hands in his pockets. Feeling more compact, more detached and alone, he walked down the street through alternating patches of light and shadow. The cold made everything look clear and crisp, including the light from the street lamps.

At the corner, a homeless man approached him. Roberto stood motionless and stared at the man's long face and mottled complexion. The streetlight accentuated the wrinkled face, and gave the white hair a sandy appearance. An outstretched calloused hand revealed bony fingers and long unkempt nails. Roberto's heart beat faster and drops of sweat sprouted on his forehead. The beggar's odor made his proximity intolerable and evoked a childhood memory. At a Sunday Mass, an old woman had sat next to him, her skin hanging in folds reeking of decay. At the end of the service, he had rushed out of the church gasping. The memory remained vivid.

Now, he bolted down the street to reach the sanctuary of Anna's apartment. He imagined her wearing a yellow sweater and black ski pants stretched tightly over her thighs. He looked forward to being greeted with a hug. She would sit next him, her head on his shoulder, and she would make idle talk about the day. The dimly lit room would, like an infinitely gentle and powerful guardian, embrace them both.

In the summer they had lain together in the grass and gazed at the sky, and when a breeze blew through the leaves of the trees they had watched them scintillate in the sunlight. He recalled a green field in Central Park covered with yellow flowers, and he and Anne counted the petals until both were too tired to continue and lost count. Then, he picked flowers and put them in her hair. All these things he remembered, but he especially remembered her contour against the rocks beneath Belvedere Tower, her white soft skin against the grain of the hard minerals, or from a little distance, her silhouette behind which loomed the tower, a small castle perched on the rocks overlooking the lake.

He ascended the brightly lit narrow stairway to her door. He knocked, but no one answered. Distraught, he again walked out to the street, crossed to the other side and glanced back at the gray cluster of buildings. Why had she agreed to see him, if she wasn't going to be home? Not even a note on the door. He stopped at the corner bar and ordered Bacardi. At the next table, four young people were asked for proof of age, and they each produced an ID card, except for one of the girls who proceeded to share the drinks ordered by the others. Roberto listened to the young people's conversation. One of the girls talked about bathing by candlelight, and she described how to fix the candle into the soap niche on the wall. They all thought the idea humorous and laughed. The conversation brought up the image of Anna and made Roberto feel more alone. There had been times when she had been very obliging, had kept up his morale, and was the only person he could turn to when a fit of depression enveloped him.

One of the boys took off his shoes, and in his socks went to the men's room. The waiter brought Roberto his drink, and he sipped it as he watched the shoeless boy return to play the buffoon as he looked for his shoes, which the others had hidden while he was in the restroom. Having finished his drink, Roberto got up to leave. The boy had found his shoes and had sat down in the midst of the general mirth. Roberto walked out to the street, and the young people's laughter faded behind him. He would visit his parents after all.

§

He did not expect to find another visitor, but Arturo was there, already tipsy when Roberto arrived. Mrs. Rubio was desperately trying to get the old man to go home, while Mr. Rubio, sitting on the sofa beer can in hand, enjoyed the superiority of one still in control of his faculties.

The heavy smell of human breath mixed with alcohol emanated from Arturo's shrunken figure to surround Roberto and make him feel dizzy. The old man placed his hand on Roberto's shoulder before Roberto could do anything to

avoid contact. Roberto turned his face away wishing he had
stayed away, but now he was trapped.

Tears rolled from Arturo's upturned eyes as he rambled
through sentimentalities, his protruding lower lip twitching
as he spoke. Under his graying hair, he had a long face;
sunken cheeks, his lower lip stuck out considerably, his eyes
always sad like those of a hound. His whole face, grotesquely
comic and pathetically bestial, evoked in Roberto pity and
disgust. Many times he had watched his father mimic the
effeminate mannerisms of the little man to the applause of
assembled company. On those occasions, everyone enjoyed
the joke, except Roberto's mother who quietly deplored the
callous humor.

Roberto longed for the solitude of his own apartment.
He would stay only long enough to please his mother. But
when he was about to leave, Arturo sprung to his feet to
delay the departure. Tears rolled down the little man's red
face contorted in a pathetic expression. "You know, Roberto,
you know how I always thought of you as a son. Like a
son, Roberto! I'm an old man, Roberto, and I have nobody,
nobody at all. My parents died when I was a boy, my very
own parents. I have nobody, Roberto, nobody!"

Roberto propped himself up against the wall trying to
hide his disgust while Arturo babbled his life story in a plea
to be rescued from his loneliness.

Perspiration covered Roberto's face. The smell of
brilliantine in Arturo's hair, mixed with the alcohol from
his breath worked its way into Roberto's lungs, and the
smell transformed into a taste, as if his mouth were coated
with castor oil. He longed for a breath of fresh air. "Your
miserable life is not my fault!" he wanted to shout at the old

man. He wanted to spit out the bad taste, but his mouth felt dry. He would have collapsed had his mother not intervened and drawn Arturo away.

Roberto quickly said goodbye and left. When he got home, he lay on his bed and for a long time wondered what tomorrow would bring.

# Chicken Curry

*F**ROM THE SOUND* of the gunfire, O'Hara could tell that there were at least three snipers on the other side of the river, maybe more. He could send a patrol to cross downstream and come up behind them, but that was too obvious. They would be expecting that. Besides, it would take too long. He needed helicopter support.

"O'Hara, we don't have any fuck'n helicopters available right now."

"Okay, Captain," he said. "It's going to take forever to cross the river if we don't come up from behind."

"God damn it, O'Hara, do your job and spare me the details."

"Yes sir, Captain," O'Hara said out loud, with "Go fuck yourself," under his breath. He put down the field telephone and took out his map in the hope that a closer scrutiny of it would suggest a plan by which to get himself and his men out of the predicament. They had been in worse situations, but he did not want to think about those. This one was bad enough, and its relative standing was not going to make it any easier. Stay with the moment was the cardinal rule. The minute you got lost in the past or dreamed about the future your chances of surviving diminished. O'Hara knew that well enough.

Downstream was the easiest place to cross. Upstream there was a sharp incline, and rough terrain before one could reach the rear of the enemy position. O'Hara reasoned that if the enemy were shorthanded, they would set the ambush downstream, and even if they weren't, they would do it, thinking that the Americans would take the easy way out. Just like gooks to think that way, O'Hara thought. If we wanted the easy way out, we wouldn't be here at all. They are right in one respect—we're not smart enough to take the easy way out. At least I'm not, O'Hara said to himself.

"Gibson, Morales, get your asses over here, we're taking a little hike."

"You going too, Lieutenant?" asked Gibson, whose real name was Julio Torres but for some reason, still a mystery to O'Hara, was always called Gibson.

"Looks that way, doesn't it, Gibson?"

"Sure does Lieutenant. You're one hell of a guy," Gibson said with a straight face.

That was the one thing that was irksome about Gibson. O'Hara could never tell when Gibson was putting him on. Otherwise he was a first rate soldier, which had come as a surprise to O'Hara, who prided himself on being a good predictor of who would do well in the field and who would wash out, a knack he had developed to insure his own survival. Ninety-nine percent of the time he was right. Gibson, however, was part of the one percent that always surprised him.

O'Hara had pegged Gibson as a thinker the minute he laid eyes on him. Thinkers ended up dead more often than not, either that or deserting, which was tantamount to the same thing as far as O'Hara was concerned. Thinkers didn't do the kind of thinking that kept you alive. They did the kind of thinking that kept you from reacting fast enough. Everything happened in their conscious minds first and foremost, and life was only a shadow of their dreams. O'Hara had no use for that kind of person. Maybe they had a place somewhere in the scheme of the universe, but not in soldiering. O'Hara was sure of that, and that was a comfort to him, because every day he was less and less sure of the certainties he had cherished before he had come to this war.

Gibson had fooled him though. At first everything had gone the way O'Hara though it would. Then something had happened. O'Hara had not been able to figure out what it was that had changed Gibson, but something had awoken him—transformed him into a hunter swift and sure. O'Hara had seen that happen a few times before, usually when a guy had seen a buddy killed in a particularly unpalatable way; then rage could transform a man, sometimes forever, sometimes only for a while. But Gibson was a loner; he had no buddies. He was friendly enough, easy to get along with, but he wasn't anybody's buddy. Friendship implied an emotional attachment. Transitory as such attachments might be among soldiers, they are still real and necessary. But Gibson kept himself apart.

Death did not shake him up the way it did other people. That was part of his strangeness, part of what O'Hara did not understand about him. Still, he turned out to be a good soldier. He obeyed orders and did his job without complaint, and he had a talent for hunting the enemy, for anticipating his move. A seasoned soldier becomes adept at these things, but Gibson's experience was too limited for that. Perhaps in another life he had been a soldier, but in this one, he had only been at the front two months before O'Hara had noticed the change. Everybody changes in combat; at some point you're not a greenhorn anymore, but that was not the kind of change O'Hara had seen in Gibson. Gibson's change had been the awakening of a talent.

O'Hara, Gibson, and Morales went upstream to ford the river where the enemy would least expect.

"How far up we gonna go, Lieutenant? They may have a whole fuck'n division up there. We'd have to go up pretty far to get behind them. Then three of us ain't gonna be much use."

"We're going up about a mile. If we run into any patrols, we'll have to determine whether we should proceed with the plan or turn back."

"It's gonna take us a couple of hours to go a mile in this bush," Morales said.

"So let's get going already," Gibson said.

From the other side of the river the sound of gunfire kept coming, and mortar response didn't seem to have any effect. Gibson took the point first. In a while he would switch with Morales. That way they could rest alternately as they cut through the underbrush. O'Hara also took turns, because he wanted to show that he was every bit as fit as every one of his men, especially Gibson. He liked Gibson, he told himself. There was nothing to dislike about him, but O'Hara worried that Gibson was the kind of guy that would show him up. O'Hara didn't like that in himself.

It is an axiom of command that good men make their commanders look good, and O'Hara knew full well that it was an asset to have Gibson under his command. But O'Hara could not get rid of the competitive feeling that made him constantly measure himself against Gibson. He did not want to do it. He had not done it often before, not since high school when Peter Larouche had emerged as a star quarterback to rival O'Hara's position. They played on the same team, but O'Hara had found himself wishing that Larouche would throw a wild pass once in a while. He had gotten beyond that. It was one of the milestones of his life when he realized that Peter's abilities did not detract from his own. "Do your best," his father had said. "That's all a man is required to do." O'Hara strove to do that.

Across the river only the jungle rising straight up from the bank was visible. The water in the river was light brown like coffee with a great deal of milk in it. It was a river of coffee flowing down through a green tropical forest, but there was no smell of coffee. There was only the smell of the forest and the smell of the river. Along the bank, where the river met the forest, mingled the smell of decay. The forest was a contradiction. Decay on the ground sustained the plush life that reached out to the sky. There was death and danger everywhere as each living thing strove to survive at the expense of something else, and yet the total effect of it was an overabundance of life.

The three men cut their way up the river to a point where they could cross. The difficult work made them perspire profusely, so that their clothes were as wet as if they had been walking in a shower of warm rain. The rain in the tropics was always warm. It was soothing. That was a nice thing about the tropics—warm rain. In New York the rain was cold, so that if you walked in the rain and got drenched, you would get chilled to the bone even in August. In the tropics, the rain was warm and soothing, and it was relaxing to walk in the rain. At the moment, they were wet from perspiration and not from the rain, but they were nevertheless wet, so that wading into the river would not make a big difference. They made a raft for their gear and towed it across as they swam. The current was mild, but the river was wide. They reached the other side a little below where they had intended but close enough.

The killing time close, O'Hara intently watched his two companions to make sure they were prepared for what they had to do. Everyman behaved differently before combat, and sometimes the same man behaved differently each time. Morales was always nervous. He was afraid to die. Before a battle he always obsessed about the possibility of death or injury. He clutched the crucifix of the rosary he always wore around his neck then he crossed himself. He never failed to do that before going in to kill. Watching him, Gibson conceded that it was all right to pray. It was conceivable that the Cisco Kid carried in his saddlebag an ebony rosary, a carefully wrought silver Christ against a black cross. There was no evidence to the contrary.

"Wake up, Gibson! What are you dreaming about?"

"Cowboys," he said.

"You like rodeos?"

"Never been to a rodeo. I was thinking of the first TV show I ever saw, the Cisco Kid."

"Shit, he wasn't a real cowboy, just a wetback."

"Sure, Lieutenant, anything you say."

Gibson checked his weapon. He checked his gear to see that everything was in place. He was ready. He watched Morales do his little ritual with the crucifix. He didn't begrudge him that. Whatever worked was all right, and if the crucifix worked for Morales, so be it. It was a way of getting rid of the fear. The fear made you do things that were unpredictable and that you knew were the wrong things to do even as you did them. So it was imperative to get rid of the fear in any way that worked. The rosary worked for Morales partially, but the fear never left him entirely. It shrunk to a very small area, and there he kept it under control, but he could still feel it in his gut. He kept the fear small, but it was there like a seed waiting to grow under the right conditions.

Gibson had fear also, but he kept his fear in his head. There it was easier to control than if it were in some other part of the body. Gibson made friends with his fear. Death was not the enemy. Death was part of the life that he was living at the moment. He accepted it. Death was not altogether a bad thing. Only pain was bad. Gibson did not want to die in pain. He had procured on the black market a supply of cyanide capsules, some of which he kept on his person at all times. Gibson had accepted the possibility of his own death; or rather, he had accepted the inevitability of it. He counted himself no longer among the living and that freed him from the need to fear. Death had no horror for him, and he had no regrets about his life. He had lived it the best that he could, every minute of it aware of his own becoming.

The forest ground was always wet. It was a place where the sun had no dominion. Gibson felt the moistness of the ground as he crawled toward the enemy. The ground was a friendly place. To have as much of one's body as possible touching the ground was a comforting feeling, just like having his body up against a woman was a comfort. Perhaps, like Antaeus, he would get strength from touching the ground. Gibson understood that myth now. Perhaps children understand it also, he thought. They are so often close to the ground. But when do grown men crawl on the ground except when they are doing something thoroughly unnatural like trying to kill each other. The ground was moist, and soon he would add to its moisture by spilling the blood of the enemy, or maybe his own blood would be on the ground. He might be killed; then he would be put in the ground somewhere. Eternal rest they called it, but it was no such thing. It was only nothingness. To rest, one had to be alive; to enjoy the closeness of the earth, one had to be alive. Death was nothingness, and nothingness was only a concept. It could not be felt.

He could see the enemy now through the foliage. He could see them moving about unsuspecting that death was imminent. In Gibson's mind they were no longer real men, only shadows of men, just as he was also. When they had decided to hunt each other they had left the world of the living to become shadows. Gibson understood that, and he had no fear. He was close now, too close to crawl any further. Now he had to stand up, because he could not leap on his prey from a crawling position. A cat could do that and have the advantage in this hunting game. He was not a cat. He was a man, and a man needed to be on his two feet to pounce.

When he stood up, he became aware of his vulnerability. At the critical point, there was distance between him and the earth. His body responded; his heart beat faster; his nerves became more sensitive. The slightest alarm would have set him off, as he waited for the right moment. He would know the moment almost instinctively, but he prepared for it nevertheless. In slow motion, the scenario ran through his mind frame by frame. The key to flawless execution was visualization. Gibson and Morales could go in hand to hand while O'Hara covered them in case anything went wrong. Hopefully there would be no firing, so that the main force by the river would not be alerted.

Gibson looked over at Morales to check that he was in position. They looked into each other's eyes and each saw that the other was ready. This was it, the ultimate trust. Each life depended on the other. Gibson gave the signal, and they sprang into action. By O'Hara's reckoning the fray was over in an instant, but to Gibson it seem interminable. Success depended on the swiftness of the knife, but the knife seemed made of rubber. The smell of a man close up as he was about to die was always unpleasant to Gibson, and that was the one thing that he could not get used to, but there was no escaping it. He could not hold his nose nor even turn away his head. The only remedy was to dispatch the man as quickly as possible and drop him. There was closeness there too, a closeness in killing, a certain intimacy unusual among men. After the killing there was loneliness, but the execution provided closeness.

"You all right, Morales?" Gibson asked.

"I'm all right," he said. He didn't look all right.

"We have to go on," Gibson said.

O'Hara came into the clearing. "Let's go before they get wind of this."

Morales looked green. "This guy is not dead yet," he said.

"Finish him off," O'Hara said.

"Can't do it with a knife," Morales said.

"Why not?"

"I just can't," he said. "You plug him."

"Leave him then."

"He'll die slowly. It's not right."

"Let's go, we're wasting time."

"Can't leave him there in pain."

"Why not? He'd do it to you," O'Hara said.

"I'll take care of it," Gibson said.

"How are you going to do it?" Morales asked.

Gibson took out one of his cyanide capsules.

"You guys are crazy," O'Hara said.

"Maybe so," Gibson said. He knelt by the side of the dying man and put the capsule between his teeth then he pushed the chin up. It was a waste of a good cyanide capsule. He was only doing it for Morales. They needed Morales yet for a while, until they got to the river. Morales was becoming unhinged, Gibson could see it, so he would shore up Morales for a little while. It was the only thing to do. It was practical, but also he liked Morales. Gibson hoped that Morales would make it through to the end of the detail. Maybe he would get wounded bad enough to be sent home. It was better than getting killed. Morales would get killed if he stayed in the front much longer, but now was not the time to think about that. They had to get to the river and finish the killing. Gibson's blood was racing now, and he wanted to get to the river while he was still in a killing mood. It would be easier at the river, because they would use their automatics. No need to get close up, no need to smell the enemy. There would only be the acrid smell of gunpowder.

The sound of birds was gone from the forest. There was only the sound of gunfire and mortar. The three hunters moved in on their prey unnoticed. They had spread out about twenty yards apart. They had spied out where the bulk of the enemy was. For sure they would get most of them in the first rush. Then they would have to be fast and alert to clean up. The few seconds after the first strike were the most dangerous. Whatever enemy was still alive would try to make his death count.

O'Hara was going down the middle. He could signal to both Gibson and Morales. When he gave the go ahead, they all three ran forward firing as they went. The bodies of the snipers fell from the trees like coconuts from palms. The firing was continuous. The men advanced behind a wall of bullets. Across the river the rest of the platoon, realizing that the rear action was in progress, began to advance. Caught in the crossfire, the enemy had no chance to withdraw.

§

Gibson sat on the ground between the roots of a tree, his back up against the trunk. He held his M16 between his legs, the barrel pointing to the sky. His hair was wet with perspiration, and his body ached from exertion. He took a candy bar from his pack and munched on it with his eyes closed. Eating was one of the few good things left in this life of killing. Eating made him think of women who were far away and whom he would in all probability never see again. He thought of a woman whom he had once loved. She had been tall and graceful and very charming. She had cooked chicken curry for him with all the chicken taken off the bones. He remembered the taste of the chicken and the curry and the raisins. Sometimes he dreamed of eating chicken curry like she had made that day, but he never bothered to look for the recipe, and there was never chicken curry like that in restaurants. Sitting against the tree, his face dirty and his body aching, he thought of chicken curry sprinkled with shredded coconut, until Morales's voice brought him back to reality.

About twenty feet away, crying and muttering words to Jesus Christ, Morales stood over the body of one of the enemy, a boy fifteen or sixteen years old with bullet wounds down from his chest to his pelvis.

"This can't be," Morales was saying to himself.

Gibson considered going over to Morales and comforting him, but he thought better of it. Morales was beyond comfort. He would die soon. It was not smart to get involved with the dead. Gibson closed his eyes and resumed his reverie. He could almost taste the chicken curry.